Due

Season

Dr. Pat Dugas

B D B Publishing, Unltd.

Decatur, Georgia 30032

BDB Publishing, Unltd.

2031 Rockhaven Drive

Decatur, Georgia 30032

Library of Congress Catalog Card Number: 88-071454

ISBN: 0-925-02200-4

First B D B Printing: 1992

Second B D B Printing: 2015

Printed in the U.S.A.

DUE SEASON

BY: Dr. Pat Dugas
DUE SEASON IS . . .

Technology may well be the main reason that book clubs do not appear too popular these days. In times past, their existence would provide opportunities for readers to discuss a book's contents. Additionally, authors would, sometimes, visit these club meetings. Of course, this would enable the reader to ask why certain characters made various choices and decisions, as well as question outcomes. Conversations with the author may question if there were any hidden agendas or conclusions that could, or should be formed . . . whether there was an actual hero or villain, etc.

With these possibilities afloat, the author of <u>Due Season</u> decided to share a few observations and revelations that gave rise to its inception. Initially, the author was confused and even upset, as she witnessed life happening. There seemed to have been an astronomical number of sad and rude people with negative attitudes and vindictive spirits.

Studying the Bible provides answers to its audience. But, there remain many others who shy away, because they claim it is difficult reading. The King James Version affords a beautiful read, but its users are often left with a need for further investigation. The Amplified, NIV and Message Bibles are three examples of the many modern day translations that help Word seekers accomplish their missions.

Contrary to popular opinion, multiple members of our society are desirous of helping others transform their brokenness. Ministers of the Gospel are, constantly, reassuring their congregations that Jesus promised to be their companion, victory, resource, energy and anointing.

If you agree as a minister, seminarian, Bible student, or lay person, that intercessors are needed, you will, especially appreciate this pontification of unwholesome AND wholesome living. Read and compare the quality of life for each.

Seminaries define "apologetics" as "a systematic discourse, establishing or defending a Bible doctrine." Utilizing the aforementioned device, this author, after having received Divine Guidance, penned this story. Hopefully, it will help others find their way and accomplish goals.

By no means is this author, strictly, interested in developing ministers, as the primary purpose of <u>Due Season</u>. More so, Dr. Dugas has embraced the paraphrased axiom, "May the unburned take the advice of the burned." (See Luke 16:9)

This author likens the way humans live to a garden and the planter / farmer. It is implied that if one plants tomatoes, the gardener should NOT expect onions to grow. Similarly, it is unfeasible for the seeds to produce a ready harvest the very next day. Rather, when Father God sends sunlight and rain, the potential crop discovers what it needs for manifestation.

Another productive notation is that portions of a garden may come from seedlings, while others grow from actual seeds. Those

4

that come from seeds, frequently, begin their lives in incubation – in the gardener's house (or greenhouse). This process provides nurturing – safety from animals and inclement weather.

When the gardener is ready to actually plant, in anticipation of a crop, he must have pre-decided which area constitutes "good ground," for growth. (See Luke 8:8, KJV). As one pastor stated, "Otherwise, they will NOT develop to their full potential."

When this novel was first published in 1992, Dr. Dugas referenced Galatians 6:9 as the main Scripture of inspiration:

> Let us not be weary in doing good, for at the <u>proper</u> <u>time</u> we will <u>reap a harvest</u> if we do not give up (NIV).

> So let's not allow ourselves to get fatigued doing good. At the <u>right time</u> we will <u>harvest a good crop,</u> if We don't give up, and quit (The message).

> And let us not be weary in well doing: for in <u>due season</u> we shall <u>reap,</u> if we faint not (KJV).

According to the eighth chapter of Luke, Mankind is confronted with which type of ground he wants in his garden, daily. Included in those choices are four types: wayside, rock, thorns and good ground.

Wayside is hard and rough; water and seeds cannot sink in. (The cold-hearted, people with bad attitudes and nasty personalities help make up this body. These people provide Satan with the opportunity to steal the Word from their hearts).

Rocky soil is too thick for seeds to take root. The seeds may sprout, but they will wither away. (When the storms of life come, there is no anchor).

Thorny soil smothers seeds; their surroundings choke life – living water – from the plants. (Negativity / thorns / a briar patch can be in the person of a family or church member, neighbor or co-worker).

Good ground provides nutrients for a healthy and wholesome harvest. (These people are often referred to as "saints." They are in touch with the Will of Father God, realizing that His Way is filled with possibility).

Due Season provides its readers with exposure to all types of people, places and choices. And, since Father God is no respecter of persons, the reader has the benefit to watch results unfold. The characters are black, white, male, female, older, indigent, middle class and wealthy. They all make choices and reap, accordingly.

IN APPRECIATION

With sincere appreciation to Rev. David Cotton and family, Deacons Moore (Dr. Debra) and Hurst (Detrich) and "Buddy." To Dr. Corine Wilson and Staff, Sorors Gloria and Sister, Elsie, Julia, Sonda, Bonita and their families.

Special Posthumous thanks to Ann and Papa Dugas.

And, thanks to my readers for sharing these revelations.

Spiritual Guidance / Enlightenment

Home, Rev. Isaac "Ike" Brown*, Greater Mt. Calvary Baptist Church (where my parents met and married), Rev. B. J. Johnson (Sr.* and Jr.) Bishop Dr. Corneilius Henderson,* Andrews Chapel U. M. Church, Shiloh Baptist Church, Sts. Peter and Paul Catholic Church, the Boddies, Sis. Odessa Dansby*, "Monie," Sheryl, Rev. Lewis Linsey, Rev. J. Guyton, Ken and Gloria Copeland, Dr. Charles Stanley, Apostle Mary Turner and Pastor T, Rev. Albert Lindsay and Pastor Jerry D. Black.

The Rich Journey

Irvin, Smith, and Mill Streets and Whiteline Drive families; the music community: G. G.* and Alfred, Bernice Dorsey Johnson*, Mr. Bostic*, Ron Ellis and "Prof," Mr. Buster Freeman's entrustment; my big sister, Carolyn Crowder (Atlanta School Board veteran); my little sister, Robert and Felicia Miles and family, Alfred Clay and family, Stephanie Turnipseed, and their families; Daddy's and Mama's first: Mattie* and Madalyn,* their families; The Honorable J. E. "Billy" McKinney*, and Honorable Betty J. Clark*; family of and Honorable David Scott, the Schadls, Dr. Charles Johnson, Dr. Malcolm Polk, Dr. Mary J. Thomas and Gladys Johnson's encouragement, Doug, M. L., Rolfe, B. G. Rootes, Jerome, Mary W., Jackie, Eddie and Dr. Reeves; "Super Lou," of the Hawks, Jonesboro Elementary School, Mrs. R. T. Smith*, Miss Arnold*, staff and alumnae/alumni.

W. A. Fountain High School, Mr. M. D. Roberts*, Mrs. Eula (Ponds) Perry*, Mr. Eddie White, Mrs. J. Holt*, staff and alumnae/alumni.

Fort Valley State University, Dr. C. V. Troup*, Dr. W. W. E. Blanchet,* William L.* and Henri (Avent) Dugas*, Dr. Earl Pierro*, Dr. Robert Threatt, Dr. S. E. Rutland*, Dr. Robert Steele, Dr. Ozias Pearson, "Prof" Adams and the "Marching Wildcats" (Sherry, Brenda*, Frank W. Rick, Billy D* and Me), the Peachite staff, the English Department (ESP. Dr. Doris Adams, Dr. "Jan" Green Bryant, Mrs. "Lou" Powell, Mr. Joe Adkins* - Drama, Mrs. Elaine Douglas*,

Frank M., Betty and Nikki); Coaches Hawkins*, Lomax, and their families, staff and alumnae/alumni.

Georgia State and Clark – Atlanta Universities, Life Christian University, and Living Water Bible Seminary.

And, finally, my fellow "Golden Girls" (Thanks, Wade, Jr.): Dr. Jacque George, Brenda Hinton, and Patricia Green: "Gullie," Reverend Dr. Carolyn Tarrant, Johnnie Evans, Julia Jordan, Velma Meade, Denise Smith, Venus Lewis, "Dot" Daniels (Miss Delta), Dr. B. B. Montgomery, Dr. Lorraine Walton, and their families, including my beautiful Sisters of Eta Phi Beta Sorority, Inc. (Sonda Bradfield, Basileus, Gamma Theta Chapter, Atlanta, Ga.) The Honorable David and Alfredia Scott, Dr. Charles Johnson, Dr. Malcolm Polk, Rhunell Norrington Walker and Family.

*Posthumous Recognition

With Sincere Appreciation

This book honors, posthumously, my parents, Deacon (Coach) Julius and Mother Ella M. Brown. They persevered and served as role models to their own children and grandchildren, as well as neighbors and church members. In addition to material contributions, they shared love, guidance and prayers.

Gratitude explodes to the many people and institutions that believe and teach that life boomerangs in season, as Apostle Paul teaches in Galatians 6:9. This is the Scripture whose theme is modeled in the story you are about to read.

Eternal thanks to my daughter (minister and professional writer), Rev. Dr. Candi Dugas, who blessed my life in a multitude of ways, and my granddaughter, Jordan Alexis Crawford, who remains the center of my joy. To the multitude of students whose lives were intertwined with mine for more than thirty-three years, in the classroom and beyond. This memorializes my friends, relatives and acquaintances that trusted my revealed purpose and ability to transfer and transform into understandable print. This is inclusive of Sue Ellen James, her family and classmates (my very first homeroom and senior English class, after I graduated from Fort Valley State University).

My neighbors, the Walkers, Clarks, Derrichos and Jackson families, Deacon & Mrs. Nat Harris (Sherry).

And, finally, to the ones whose influences weigh heavily on my daily choices: Both sets of grandparents (the Carters and Browns) and all ancestors. I can never forget Bishop Cornelius Henderson, Dr. and Rev. B. J. Johnson, Sr. and Jr., Papa (Rev. Isaac Brown) and Momma Nervie, the Arnold sisters, Em, Aunt Johnnie, Mrs. Perry (Ponds), Billy, Mama and Papa Dugas, L. Rae and Bei Lei, Dr. John Mobley and Open Campus High School.

There are innumerable friends who continue to be encouraging, especially (Emridge and Iyinka), Lady Kate and the Women's Ministry (Sisters Paula Neely and Patsy Thompson, Reverends Byrd and Hoover, et al) Mrs. Cathrine Starr and Family, Bettie D. Scott, Hassie L. Buckner, Pat Roberson Fickling, Melody Riggins and Gerri Lawrence. I am grateful for the countless sermons of guidance and inspiration by Pastor Jerry Black, Reverends Parison and Seals and their families, other associate ministers and my entire beloved Beulah Family and its VBS. The current staff and students at E. Andrews High School and Mr. M. Jones, principal, who are sketched on my heart, will reign among fond memories. Mark Kelmachter and Yolanda Dawan remain in the count. Inclusive of long-standing relationships are Janet Broughton Slaughter and her children, Jeanette Turnipseed Crowder and family, Howard and Stephenie Turnipseed (my niece), Angela Johnson, Darryl Crowder, Tereon Crowder, Arre and Sabrina Kennedy, Katrina Crowder Ingram and family, Willie H. Brown and Carolyn Crowder, Joyce Souder Pritchard, the Golden Girls from my childhood. They are Dr. Jacquelyn Souder George, Mrs. Patrica Askew Green and Mrs. Brenda Minnitee Hinton, Reverend Dr. Carolyn J. Tarrant (former college roommate).

I am indebted to LWBS/Life Christian University (Apostle Mary Turner and husband, Overseer Anthony Turner, Ministers Hamm and Melanie Dudley), the Family Life Center at Beulah and its "bid whist" component. Others who were encouraging include Dale Hill, the Gilyards, Chris Hightower, Harriett Reedy, Dr. Bobby (Portia) Griffin, Dot Jenkins, Annie Ramey, Julia Edwards, Reverend and Mrs. Freddy McCray (Brenda), Rev. Strozier, Rev. and Mrs. Edwards (Marilyn), Rev. and Mrs. Chapman, Reverend Angela Solomon, Deacon Jacques (Gerri) Ricks, Linda Denmark, Glenda Williams, Dr. Donna, "Miss Mary" and the Wrecking Crew, Ms Jean, Chip and family, Minister and Mrs. Pembroke and family, the Sunday School (Deacon King and Mike Moore) and Deacon Phil and Dr.

Agnes McGregor, Fray White, Dr. Barbara Winters, Mrs. Gloria Hankerson Artis, Minh Luu and GPS, Mr. and Mrs. Moses Brewington, Vivian Bonner, Yolanda Dawan and Debra Dixon.

The final group of loving, encouraging and productive contributors consists of my new classmates, from Senior Strength-Training, with "Dr. Nick" (Dominic Jefferson), who feeds our physical AND Spiritual needs. He provides positive growth potential with encouragement and hope. They are: Martha Sims, Cynthia H. Tucker, A. Jean Smith, Albertha Daniel, Loveday Wright, Doris B. Hamilton, Rose Brown, Mildred Hill, "Ida," Carlestine Hart, Ida Fambrough, Carol E. Ramseur, Mary Ramseur-Tatum, Robin Anthony and Deborah Dykes.

Dedication

It is with utmost pleasure and honor that I dedicate this novel to one who managed to leave everyone she knew with the impression of being her "best friend." What joy the Beulah Community Family Life Center enjoyed, as she greeted and inquired about the health of its members by name. Of course, the inquiry included our parents, children and their accomplishments.

The ONLY reason some of us were privy to the heroic saga in which she starred, we asked. This is how we learned that NOT ONLY was she the custodial parent to her own biological children, but lovingly included the child her deceased sister left behind. She assumed this responsibility when the mother passed away at an early age, in 1993.

Indeed, she was quite exemplary of the valuable woman described (and often talked about on Women's Day celebrations) in wisdom from the Book of Proverbs. Not only did she provide a "roof and a bed," this woman of God led by example. She earned an education, and all the children fell close to "the tree."

Additionally, she attended early morning service at her beloved Beulah Missionary Baptist Church, under the Tutelage of Reverend Jerry D. Black. She was retired from AT&T, a member of The Golden Eagles and an usher, both with the attitude of service.

Carrie Winfrey Roney was so connected to her Lord and Savior that even her daughter would question (what appeared to be) her "don't care attitude." But, what the daughter witnessed was her mother's profound faith. In fact, her favorite Bible verse was, "Do not be anxious about anything, but in every situation, by prayer and petition, with thanksgiving, present your requests to God," located in Philippians 4:6.

Carrie's friend, co-worker and travel companion, Jan Martin, described her as one to be adored, admired and trusted. She was so impressive that Jan often wondered why she was blessed to have such a "model" as a best friend. Carrie led by example and refused to put others "down." This trait inspired Jan to be a better person. She stated that most people knew that, "Carrie didn't treat everybody the same, but she treated everybody right." The photo (of Carrie and Jan) below demonstrates the bonds this amazing woman developed with EVERYBODY, if one would dare cross her path.

Nick, Anthony & The Family Life Center,

We know how you felt about her, but please allow us to share how she felt about you. Our mother had more than one career, but the center was truly her joy and passion. To the card players, the members at the front desk, and every other outlet of the Family life Center: We thank you so much. You all gave her life, and we will never forget the bond of the Life Center. We could go on and on about how much she loved the Center. Instead, we simply say thank you!

As we find strength from your prayers and ours to face the days ahead by leaning on God's everlasting arms we want you to know that we are thankful for your expressions of sympathy during the passing of our mother.

THE FAMILY OF
Carrie Winfrey Roney
CELESTE R. RONEY
CLAUDE R. RONEY JR.
COLLEY WINFREY

"Don't worry about anything; instead pray about everything.
Tell God what you need, and thank him for all he has done."
Philippians 4:6

Counted among the Multitudes was her loving "Bid Whist" Club, listed alphabetically: Sam Alexander, Earlene Anderson, Pearl Anderson, Charles Bagsby, Andrew Barnes, Leroy Brewer, Moses Brewington, Herman Brown, Rose Brown, Fran Camp, Ruby Canty, Barbara Carey, Arthur Carlisle, Dennis Cofer (our resident angler), Linda Denmark, Pat Dugas, Leroy Ellington, Leo Fickling, John Flen, Jerry Flint, Charles and Carolyn Floyd, Bobby Griffin, Charlie Henderson, Doug Henry, Dale Hill, Mildred Hill, Otis Houston, Walter Houston, Coleman Jackson, Alan Jones, Brenda Knox, Anthony Love, Leroy Major, Jan Martin, Jesse Cox, Jerald Moore (Butch), Terry Nelson, Willie Mae Nelson, Gene Odom, William Oliver, Bernard Pattillo, Cliff Roberts, Charles Robinson, Jacques Ricks, Melody Riggins, Ada Sadler, Ed Stephens, Sidney Stokes, Walter Thompson, Bill Walker, Ruby Williams and Pat Young.

CONTENTS

Foreword by Paula E. Bonds, Esquire

Prologue

Book I – COCOON -   23

Book II – ON BECOMING -   32

Book III – THE MET AMORPHOSIS -   42

Book IV – STATE OF BEING -   54

Book V The Emergence   71

Book VI – PREPARING FOR THE HARVEST   81

Book VII – THE CONTROLLING DEVICE -   107

Book VIII – BELIEF IS CRUCIAL -   113

Book IX --THE AWAKENING -   117

Book X – ON DECIDING -   123

Book XI – DUE CROSS AND CROWN -   132

Book XII – SEASON FOR THE BUTTERFLY   135

About the Author   139

Epilogue

FOREWORD

What a wonderful blessing is in store for you! Your life and consciousness are about to be touched by a truly extraordinary woman Dr. Patricia Brown Dugas.

A seeker of Truth.
A thirster after Wisdom.

A Mothering Spirit –
always giving, nurturing.

SENSITIVE
Extremely Sensitive
Exceedingly Sensitive.

able to intuit all the nuances and shadings;
able to sense the meaning behind the words,
the feeling beneath the actions.

Reflective.
Receptive.
Centered.

such gentle soul –
loving,
accepting,
caring.

like the water element other sun sign –
restful...refreshing...relaxing...soothing...
constant...therapeutic...cleansing...peaceful...
restorative...HEALING.

NEVER A HARSH OR UNKIND WORD.

always, always, ALWAYS seeing only the bright
and brighter side
of life
of people
of experiences.

Quick, even anxious, to forgive.
Responsible and Uncomplaining.
A TRUE FRIEND.
a woman of her word,
compassionate,
available,
ever willing to help,
to share,
to empathize,
to
give support.

Determined.
Hard-working.
Industrious.

Resilient.
courageously bouncing back
after the hurts, the pain the disappoints
ever moving forward,
growing,
growing wisher and stronger
but never hard, never cold.
constantly expressing her loving
essence
no matter what,
in spite of everything

STRONG,
    But a quiet, confident, ego-less strength,

        taking her share of the load and then some,
          cheerfully doing what is necessary,
            always grateful for the strength to serve,
              ever seeking the chance to do, be
                and give even more.

      a gift and dedicated Teacher; an eager
      and attentive student of life, of wise
      and positive people.
          Above all else a Spiritual person,
          a reader and DOER of the Word,
          a constant communer with the Spirit.

      Written words are her tools, her life's blood,
      her favorite communication even with the
      closest of loved ones.
          Powerfully chosen
           Effectively delivered
      Always a message to be tasted,

                  savored,
                    digested,
                      internalized.

      Yes, your lives are about to be touched –
          Thoughtfully
          Prayerfully
            Delightfully

Beautifully
LOVINGLY.

Enjoy!

Paula E. Bonds, Esq.

<u>DUE SEASON</u>

BY

DR. PAT DUGAS

PROLOGUE

"Tis a terrible thing to lie in bed and sleep not, waiting for one who cometh not, wanting to please and pleaseth not."

Book I

THE COCOON

Dearest Cissy,

This is the letter that I promised to write. How long ago has it been since our conversation – four weeks, six weeks? At that time, you asked me to detail mine and Joe's time spent together, that after two marriages, you want to know how couples can continue to live together, happily. Our activities and conversations may be totally out of character for you and this new man in your life, Patrick Donovan. Sounds like an interesting person. (To me, politicians are always fascinating). Remember, nobody is ever completely happy twenty-four hours a day, three hundred sixty-five days a year.

Unfortunately, too many women are frightened into hasty commitments, thanks to society. All I know is what my experiences have taught me. There's no magic involved. I feel that every marriage should, also, be a friendship. That way, you're better equipped for life's storms. When two people are friends and lovers, the relationship houses respect and love. "One without the other just won't do." Otherwise, all it takes is the slightest gust of wind, and it's destroyed.

You, also, said that Patrick's main drawback was his lack of humor. Somewhere, I heard that "A man who never makes a joke is a standing joke to the world."

But, if you can continue to enjoy the stolen moments of ecstasy, and admire him for what he is the world is yours. After all, Cissy, a relationship is nothing more than two people tolerating each other's weaknesses, while capitalizing on each other's strengths.

I'm your friend, so believe me when I say that what works for Joe and Chris may not work for Patrick and Cissy. It takes patience, excitement, and discovery.

Wow Cissy, our childhood was packed with excitement and startling discoveries!

***

Christine and Cissy were thirteen years old as they strolled home one night, after a walk around the block. They chose the shorter route back, through the cemetery, which was the dividing line between the Black and white communities. The north end was used for the white burials; the south end was "reserved" for Black burials.

The travelers saw the Stone's long black limousine parked under an oak tree that was located toward the central part of the cemetery. Being young and inquisitive, the girls investigated. As they approached, they could hear heavy breathing. Chris motioned to Cissy, indicating they should turn back.

Suddenly, a bottle fell from the car (one door was open), and these petrified creatures froze in their tracks. A white, nude female plunged from the car in laughter. (Cissy and Chris hid behind a shrub). The woman was mumbling about having broken her "brandy."

Momentarily, a man's voice was heard. A Black nude male appeared to retrieve his companion and calm her. A long and passionate kiss accomplished this mission. They climbed back into the car; the heavy breathing resumed. Chris and Cissy were too frightened to move; so, they remained still, hoping the passengers would take the initiative. Meanwhile, the crickets spoke their language, as the other creatures followed suit.

After what seemed an eternity had passed, the engine started. The noise caused Cissy to cry out, unnaturally! For a moment, every noise seemed to cease – the teenagers breathed, nervously. Perspiration tickled, heavily, down their brows. But, to their surprise, Cissy's cry was not heard.

The limousine skirted off in the direction of town. Shockingly, Chris and Cissy got to their feet-babbling, wildly, about their most recent encounter. As they ran home, the girls agreed to meet at the south end of "The Path," after school the next day to discuss their discovery – confirmation.

***

But, per your request, here it is. Last night, I decided to prepare an evening of excitement and adventure. As often as I get extra time, I plan a surprise for my husband, with anything exotic and different.

I selected my black sheer negligee, split on both sides, a perfect manipulator. We hadn't made love for three days, and I wanted the whole house involved in this scheme. Later, Joe found energy he swore was totally spent in his administrative capacity at the office. He works closely with a small staff, and you know how that is. Different backgrounds, individual values and jealousies, all merging and competing.

Anyway, my man came home on edge. I had called the office earlier and detected bits and pieces of the usual ongoing trivia. During those hours, he's expected to be the "Rock of Gibralta." So, as time permits, I prepare a totally different atmosphere, conducive to love, peace, and understanding.

Since I've begun to work out of the house more, I am free from office gossip.

In so doing, Joe receives encouragement and acceptance from me, which is <u>always</u> reenergizing, and his mind becomes more receptive to the positive side of life. That way, both of us benefit, now and later.

Speaking of benefiting, Joe and I went to Heaven, last night. You see, I sat in the den, downstairs, which was dark and quiet. Finally, I heard the car. I, immediately, ascended the stairway to our bedroom, which is always kept in a sexy atmosphere. I lay in a very revealing position and pretended to be asleep. I heard the garage door close; slowly, he moved toward the stairs. Each step cracked, and I found myself counting to the moment he appeared.

Tie loose, coat thrown over his left shoulder, this statute of six feet, one hundred eighty-five pounds, silhouetted at the doorway. He really looked spent; I could see his drawn face in the Shadows of light. He didn't even seem to notice my revealing pose. His jaws were tight, as though he were grinding his teeth together. It was at that moment I decided to let him know I was waiting – just for him.

I realized that my entire plan, as hard as I had worked on it, needed modifying. Joe sat on a chair and stared into the backyard, which can be rejuvenating by itself. There's a stream that flows at the extreme of our property line, and on quiet nights, one can hear the water making its way. There are just enough trees to add to the authenticity of a setting away from problems and despair.

As he stared, I walked softly toward him and began massaging his shoulders. He placed one of those big strong hands on one of mine, caressed it and said, "Baby, I thought you were asleep."

"Joe, I stayed awake for you to seduce me."

I continued the massage – all over. He said nothing, just pulled me into his lap and threw a kiss of sheer ecstasy on me. Without any more words, we communicated from heart to heart. No words were needed. Later, we showered together.

Cissy, it all boils down to Joe and me against the World. I believe any couple who makes it, sooner or later, adopts this theory, whether or not they realize it.

Sure, there are always "trapped" partners – some women, some men. But, before I got married, I decided to get a husband, not just a man to keep me, or one with whom to be seen. A husband and wife share a partnership, which is a far cry from just a marriage, a legal bind.

Don't you remember the Stone family's years of pretense and financial kingdoms? Lord, that group really caused each other pain, few triumphs – no compromises.

***

Allen K. Stone was a ruthless, aging, white businessman, whose shrewdness lent itself to magnanimous gain throughout surrounding counties in Springfield, Georgia. He adored his two children – one boy, one girl, but detested his wife, Constance. However, his wife's father represented the controlling finances behind the origin of Stone's empire. This charming giant lived his philosophy, "I never lend anything to anybody without getting something in return."

In her senior year of high school, Lisa Stone encouraged her father with an idea that gave rise to an increase in the family's financial statement.

At this time, her brother, Russell, was a senior at State, which was only thirty miles away.

Barney Blue, Russ' new running partner, was a newcomer to the south. Mr. Stone detested him on sight. Blue was Black, smart, good-looking and a native Californian, having previously been employed by a multi-billion dollar recording company.

Blue and Russ met at State College. Russ had always been a musician and was, naturally, attracted to Blue when they met, accidentally, a year ago. The visitor was a year or two older; his initial college days were interrupted by a call to serve his country. Later, he chose reserve duty, while working in PR at a recording studio. At the time, the studio was border line for bankruptcy, after having thrived years prior.

Coupled with charm and good looks, Barney Blue had graduated from high school as valedictorian. His college major had been Business Administration. Within nine months of his employment, the studio was operating inside budget. In two years, it soared to unimaginable heights.

On a rainy Monday morning, Blue met a couple who was visiting from a small town in Georgia. This mysterious twosome convinced the young explorer to investigate the professional possibilities of a group called the "Brown Clan."

After weeks of research, Blue decided to re-enroll in completion of a Bachelor's degree in Business – a perfect dual challenge.

This Georgia couple would not give Blue their home telephone number. Though the lady wore a wig and dark glasses, Blue could tell that she was a great deal older. The man was more his age and seemed to be, personally, acquainted with the members of the Brown Clan.

The couple leaned on Barney with sincerity and concern, and, the woman was especially encouraging, financially. She knew quite a few "big boys."

"After you come to town, Mr. Blue, I'll get in touch with you. When you get settled, you will be offered invitations to parties and benefits. Until then, 'Ciao'."

And, with that, the couple left the restaurant. The young man, looking back as they scurried down the street, disappeared in a taxi before Blue's car was brought around. When Blue turned again, the woman had, also, disappeared. He wondered how a small southern town felt toward such an unusually "mixed" couple.

Book II

ON BECOMING

Lisa Stone was perplexed as to how she viewed her new friend. The teenage beauty was shocked and thrilled by this foreigner's social amenities and charm. His speech was soft and jiggered. (The girl always felt like clearing her throat when he spoke). From things she heard older people say, Lisa expected Blue to be sex starved and obsessed with desire for white women. She waited.

However, Blue was always quite the gentleman in Lisa's presence. Ultimately, he was found to be her best friend, though Mrs. Stone had other plans for their guest.

On a Friday afternoon, Russ drove his partner down the long winding driveway to their triple car garage. It was raining, heavily, and Russ was glad that years ago, he had suggested automatic entrance. Though he loved the rain, he knew how fussy Blue was about his appearance. Each man, mutually, respected his friend's idiosyncrasies.

Constance Stone was home alone, chatting on the phone with Mrs. January. A cigarette was burning in the ashtray and water had accumulated at the top of her iced brandy. As was customary, Constance wore a lavender, low-cut Sassoon Original, accentuated by three gold chains of varying lengths and matching earrings. Her fingernails were carefully manicured, and fingers adorned with exquisite jewelry, having been expressly designed for the wearer.

Her son and his partner entered from the side door. Russ gestured to her, with a smile. She nodded, approvingly, and they mounted the stairs.

There was no big homecoming party, for Russ spent almost each weekend in Springfield; and on occasions, he was a visitor during the week. State College was convenient, as well as prominent.

When Constance Stone heard her son's door shut, she, immediately, informed her party that she had just been blessed with the answer to a recent prayer. She informed her caller

that it was time to have a party – the social event of the year.

Unbeknown to her friend, Connie was restless, like a caged tigress. She desired a long-awaited activity in which she, subconsciously, sought revenge, and, knowingly, sought pleasure. Her target – Barney Blue! He would be her ticket to freedom - from boredom and financial dependence.

***

Anyway, Cissy, as Joe was about to nod out, he sighed, "Baby, ten years ago, I never would've known I could be this happy and feel so complete. I thought all marriages were divorce – prone and phony."

With that, we slept, peacefully, all night long. This morning, Joe raced into preparations for work. Whistling, he started out for another day with his team. It was as though yesterday, at the office, never was.

Don't get me wrong; it hasn't always been like this. Joe is still not perfect, and neither am I. In fact, at first, I wondered if our marriage would end up in divorce court. Joe has always been his own man. He grew up hard and quick. Living in a big city where crime was rampant, he was expected to protect his two younger sisters, especially on their way to and from school. He began working at age nine. At sixteen, he had his first car accident. Out of fear, his second call was to his father.

"Hello."

"Daddy, I've had a wreck."

"Are you hurt?"

"No."

"Did you call the police?"
"Yes."
"Well, what are you calling me for?"
So many times in the past, I mistook his quiet determination and mind control for stubbornness, and I almost took his devotion and love for simplicity and lust.

It's easy for one partner to misinterpret (especially if there's little or no communication) one's actions, and reactions accordingly, often seeking revenge.

***

Constance Stone confided in her chauffeur, who confided in his sister, Catherine, that Connie continued to stay with Allen just to see him fall, that she had a plan that would make her wealthier and totally independent. Heretofore, most of Springfield looked at Allen and Connie Stone as having a successful marriage. After all, if one has money, one has everything.

From the onset, Connie's father volunteered to get Allen (an industrious young man, the son he never had) set up for success. In so doing, the old man presented this lovely couple with a completely furnished house in the middle of twelve acres, including an oasis-shaped pool, a three-lane bowling alley, billiard and game room, a spiral staircase, four levels, and a solar-roof.

The other half of Connie's dowry included her husband's initiation into the south's most prominent law firm, in which he, later, became senior partner.

Content only with making money and being powerful, Allen began neglecting his husbandly duties. Constance was, frequently, inebriated on brandy, her favorite drink. At other times, she sought solace in preparing and entertaining at parties, which Allen tolerated, gladly. That was her "hold card" and hope for control, until now.

Being Aries, Connie's way was the only way. Allen, being Leo, wanted to be the nucleus around which all things evolved. Constance spoiled her children, disgracefully. As each entered adolescence, they rebelled against their mother's possessiveness, their father's selfishness. Russ was always more adamant about his stand than Lisa. Both children were confused and frustrated.

Everybody in the Stone household had every imaginable material possession, but nobody had learned love, peace, forgiveness, or understanding. Barney Blue helped Lisa with this balance, as their friendship developed. Life, itself, taught Russ. But, their mother never got that opportunity, and their father was admitted to Lady Immaculate, a rich man's paradise for the terminally ill. Allen had stomach cancer, which was diagnosed as an ulcer, in its earlier stage.

Toward the fatal end of her life, if Constance Stone were not home reeking of brandy, she would be in bed with another man, usually Black. Her first "victim" was her chauffeur, Whitley Ronald January, whose mother was Connie's confidante from the Black community.

Christine was one of the firsts to discover this relationship when she was ten years old, soon after her parents expired.

Chris' parents were on their way home with money they had borrowed from her uncle to save their property. The father had no credit in Springfield; few Blacks did; white southern politics saw to that. Most families (both Black and white) borrowed needed monies from the Stones.

Being an attorney, Allen K. Stone familiarized himself with every possible legal loop hole to relieve the weak and ignorant of their property – from television sets to acres and acres of land. Sadly, it was all deemed legal.

A few times, some had the courage to fight, collateral, during their initial transactions. After knowledge of these tactics spread among the town's people, those who had alternatives used them. Few complained.

Christine's father was the Stones' gardener and leg man; he, also, bootlegged in the neighboring communities, with the support of his employer. Her mother never worked. Chris was an only child. And, they gained the Stone Empire at their beck and call.

When Chris was in the fourth grade, her mother informed her that surgery was needed, which could only be performed at a hospital in Alabama. Christine's father was never the man to save or prepare for rainy days. After all, Allen Stone would never allow his cohort to suffer for anything. So, when this day came, Allen's "friend" was unprepared. The month before, with Stone's help, he had just purchased a Cadillac and remodeled their house. He paid nothing down on either one. He, simply, signed a "few" papers and shook hands with Stone. Now, Chris' mother needed surgery.

Chris overheard her father on the telephone, in the kitchen, raving about how wonderful it is to have "a friend like this." He replaced the receiver, smiling. Then, he poured himself a drink and downed it in one gulp. Wiping his hands together and straightening his attire, the help-mate dashed right by his daughter to the master bedroom.

"Good news, Baby, you can stop worrying; good ole Allen has made all the arrangements. As if that's not enough, I get a month off with pay so I can be with you."

Of course, Christine's parents knew Stone's reputation, but they were an exception to the rule.

The operation was a success and all had returned to normal. When Christmas season rolled around, Chris overheard another conversation. This time, between her parents.

Since Allen was such an understanding person, Chris' father chose to spend his money, providing them with the "best" Christmas ever and making a loan payment after the incoming year. Only, he did not inform Stone of the "new" arrangement. Each night, he returned home later than before. He began staying out all night, then weekends. But, he always came home with a smile and plenty of extra cash.

Truly, Father saw to it that Christine got everything she asked for Christmas morning and plenty of things she did not ask for – like diamond earrings.

On December 26, this family trio was listening to the news when they heard a knock. It was the sheriff. Chris was too young to understand the meaning of all she heard, but somehow, it created a sickening feeling in the pit of her stomach.

Suddenly, her father began to age, and then he grew angry, followed by cries of hysteria. Christine's world seemed to be falling apart, and there was nothing she could do about it.

Before she could protest, Chris was being ushered over to the Browns, close friends of the family, for a few days. She did not mind, because she enjoyed being around such creative people. Also, next door to this family lived Catherine January, one of her classmates.

There had always been something magnetic about Cathi, and her brother was a dreamboat. He was the Stone's chauffeur. Mrs. Brown's baby sister, Cissy, who lived there was near the same age as Chris and Cathi. The girls tired each other out; at dusk, no adult had problems enticing them to sleep. After bathing, they barely made it through dinner before nodding.

Christine's parents called, daily. The fourth day, her father sounded like himself, again, promising to see her late that night, that life would be better for the small family, now. When Chris hung up, she had the strangest feeling, though she was supposed to be happier than ever.

"Mom and Dad are coming to get me tonight!"

Fate took both parents to their eternal resting place five miles outside of Springfield. They were in the curve when realizing a vehicle was approaching in their same lane. In an attempt to avoid the accident, Chris' father lost control of the car.

The child's uncle wanted her to live with him and his wife, but she did not know them. They understood and were not persistent. Her "few days" with the Browns lasted until she finished high school and moved to the town where State College was located. Chris worked on campus, utilizing her clerical skills, and for the first time in her life, sought independence. She found herself a little girl dressed in grown-ups' clothing.

"I must survive," Chris told Cissy.

Christine was making notes just before July Fourth. Plans were being made to use facilities in Springfield as a newly erected park. This park was built on a piece of land that had been swindled by Allen K. Stone, which had been a part of Russ and Lisa's estate, who donated and mandated that it be a public facility. Chris found her task both delightful and sad.

This area, when she was growing up there, was known as "The Path." It was where lovers made love at night and picnicked during the day. It was where Cissy and Chris discussed the "Cemetery Caper," so named from that frightening night when they were thirteen.

The dismissal bell, finally, sounded. Chris' homeroom teacher had been lecturing about personal hygiene, as someone had the room reeking of urine. She couldn't care less about Mrs. Mack; all she wanted was to meet Cissy at the south end of "The Path."

"Chris, I can't believe we saw Cathi's brother naked – with Mrs. Stone."
Cissy yelled this to Chris as they raced toward each other, both excited about being able to discuss the incident openly. The girls had heard rumors, but they had seen the two with their own eyes, this time. After that incident, they would often hear of the January boy

having taken Constance Stone to various long – distance engagements.

At age ten, Chris and Cissy eavesdropped a conversation between Constance Stone and April January.

(After Chris' parents expired, Allen K. Stone had taken everything they had. But, he did set up a trust fund for Christine; also, Allen provided the Browns with monthly stipends. Some said his conscience was bothering him; other speculated blackmail, having something to do with Connie and another man. Some said the other man was Chris' father that Connie had threatened to go public if Allen refused to provide for Christine).

Constance and April were in the January's living room having brandy. Catherine, Chris, and Cissy sat on the floor in the hallway, no more than six feet from the two women. What those girls heard made them, silently, depart. All three, desperately, wished they had chosen another activity. None knew how to handle this startling revelation.

**

Cissy, as I reflect on our childhood, I have fond and loving memories of your sister. Though she loved her children dearly, the two of us were never shortchanged. Perhaps I am more objective than you about Mary and Corneilius, because they are your sister and brother-in-law. Maybe you feel they were obligated to raise you, but I was just a friend's child.

Try and realize the jewel you have in your sister; talk to her about your problems and frustrations. She has a successful marriage. Anybody who has made accomplishments like another is seeking, can always, aid that person in pursuit of the same.

Don't forget, the most effective teaching method is precept and example. You can't lead where you've never been.

You've lived around Mary all of your life, and it would seem that there are certain basics you could've learned, first hand. If in doubt about your interpretations or impressions, ask her. I'm sure you'll find the results benefitting and rewarding.

***

Since adulthood, Cissy appeared to have developed more and more resentment toward Mary. The year that Mary's children (The Brown Clan) played, professionally, for the first time was in the high school gymnasium. Cissy did not want the band to play; she said there were other combos around that had more experience. Also, she made continuous catty remarks. But, the fact remained – the Clan was great!

Ultimately, Russ and Blue helped to make the Brown Clan famous. During those days, Lisa Stone would often work in PR with the guys, but she spent most of her time at the main office. Their recording studio handled the Browns, exclusively, compliments of Russ and Lisa Stone, and Barney Blue

Book III

THE METAMORPHOSIS

Blue's first trip home with Russ changed his life around, completely. As the buddies unpacked and made plans for the weekend, Mr. Stone called home. When he heard Russ had arrived, he requested a private meeting between the two of them. The patriarch had begun to experience frequent and aggravating pains in his stomach.

Five years ago, Allen K. Stone had been warned by his golf partner and trusted physician of many years, Larry Geiger, to slow down, to spend less time in court and more at the country club. But, this financial wizard strove for unreachable heights, at the expense of all, wanting, desperately, to leave his footprints in the sands of time.

"Yeah, Larry, I know. And, I'm going to rest, just as soon as I finish…"

In response to his father's summons, Russ asked Blue to keep his mother company until Lisa arrived, at which time the three young people could meet for pizza. Lisa had her own car and was visiting friends when the guys came in town. Russ left instructions with his mother to tell Lisa about bring Blue down to Chef Pizza.

Blue lay across his bed in the guest room thinking of his California connections and who he could trust as resources for his and Russ' project. Both young men knew their idea would be profitable, but neither had devised a means of selling it to the old man. And, that's what it would take – Allen K. Stone.

Little did they suspect that Lisa would provide the solution. She was a high school senior that year, and being concerned about little else, she was excited about prom night and her date.

As in a dream, an attractive, shapely woman appeared at Blue's bedside, clothed in a black bikini. Two black and white towels lay across her left arm; on the towels was a pair of trunks.

"Let's go for a swim, Barney."

The voice sounded familiar. He knew he'd heard it before. It was Mrs. Stone! The Californian got to his feet, immediately. He had been in deep thought and had not heard her enter the room. She was a beautiful woman, aging, ungracefully. Her well preserved figure made his palms wet with perspiration.

Blue fought, desperately, for control. He was startled and excited. Calmly, he said, "Sure, Mrs. Stone, but wouldn't it be better to wait for the rain to stop?"

Connie smiled, sat on the side of his bed and crossed her long, slim legs. She said nothing, just stared. The young man smiled, curiously, and sat in a chair across from his hostess.

Seductively, Connie whined, "Put your trunks on anyway."

This really made Blue excited – the idea of this charming flesh observing his. The young man acquiesced.

Walking away, Connie cooed, "Don't be shy, Barney; I have a son your age."

Just as his shorts fell to the floor, Constance reappeared with two shots of brandy.

The visitor covered his manhood with both hands. Connie almost wasted the drinks she laughed so hard.

"I don't mean to appear presumptuous, but I believe you'll need at least one hand with which to take your glass."

Barney Blue was suave, classy, good-looking, and spoiled by women. This wild attraction to him was commonplace in every circle.

"If you're sure you won't be offended."

Blue regained his composure.

With this reply, Mrs. Stone ceased laughing. She noticed a serious and concerned expression on this man's face. Not only was he lovely, she thought, he's cocky. Then, Barney became a challenge, which was even more exciting.

"My darling boy, it's sweet of you to care, but NOTHING offends me."

Directly, Blue removed both hands, took his drink, set it on the lamp table and proceeded to reach for the trunks. In mid reach, a soft hand caressed his.

Whispering, Connie revealed, "I'm going to take liberties, Barney; stop me, if you wish."

Blue's mind raced madly; his main concern was: What if Lisa comes home?

As though reading his mind, the house lady assured him that they had privacy, for she had talked to Lisa earlier. At that time, her daughter said she would call home to verify the name and number of a hair stylist before leaving her girlfriends.

This new revelation caused Blue to relax. Accordingly, his male prowess knew no bounds – no conscience. By this time, Connie had removed her two pieces and began moving toward the hallway.

Blue anticipated her next move – to lock the door. But, instead, she flipped the light switch on.

"Have you ever seen a nude white woman, Barney? If you haven't, this is new; if you have, this is old."

Constance Stone modeled her body. And, the observer beheld.

Barney Blue smiled inside, for he had been propositioned from coast to coast, by all races and both sexes. He was an extraordinary specimen, and he was respected for his manner.

The show continued, but another party joined in – the observer.

After Connie could stand the games no longer, she begged for relief.

He complied. Just as Mrs. Stone prepared for a doubleheader, the phone rang. It was Lisa.

When Constance left the room, Barney had a strange feeling that they had met before, in California.

***

Believe me, Cissy, I've really search my past and evaluated my principles, repeatedly, all in my quest for answers. When older people, in our childhood, gave advice, they neglected to be explicit. And, if questioned, they would caution you about being "sassy." However, most of their overly used quotes are beginning to hit home with me, now. One that Mary always cautioned us with was. "What goes around comes around."

Remember how students complained about Mrs. Mack, her eccentricities and her constant stream of borrowed philosophies? Well, a few years ago, I felt inclined to find her, in whatever city, just to tell her, "Thank you."

Pondering a particular course of action, I was down by the stream – staring, but not seeing – listening, but not hearing. Without warning, a soft angelic voice whispered, "Be not conformed to this world...be ye transformed by the renewing f your mind." Startled, I turned to find a pleasant expression upon the face of a plainly dressed woman.

"What?" I asked

She repeated the scripture, this time including the Biblical location.

In an attempt to be civil about such a bold invasion on my privacy, I inquired.

"Madam, are you aware that this is private property? Who are you and what are you doing here?"

The aged sojourner smiled. Strangely, I sensed an enriching closeness that I have since comprehended. Calmly, she alerted me of her involvement with a prayer band that she had knocked and rang, to no avail. As she was preparing for her departure, she detected movement in the backyard, and apologized for frightening me. My anger and fear subsided, completely; there was something soothing and magical about her voice and approach.

I invited her in, which is an extremely uncommon gesture for me.

For the first time in my life, the "living" Bible meant more than contradictions, restrictions and threats. The discussion entailed many variations. Among them, I mentioned how confusing it was, as a child, to have a problem and be lectured with adages that sounded good, but meant nothing. Specifically, one of Mrs. Mac's, "When you dig one ditch, you may as well dig two."

I told her about Allen and Connie Stone, how this one reminds me of them.

Another of the old school marm's quotes was, "Smile, and the world smiles with you; frown, and you frown alone."

Mrs. Holmes explained how people take you at your own valuation: no matter the situation, that person is responsible for his own fate.

I discovered that I was my own worst enemy; it was I, Christine, who was the guilty culprit. Furthermore, a person's frame of mind attracts its physical counterpart.

Also, Mrs. Holmes contends that anything you want to know is found in the Bible.

Her final words to me:

You were in deep thought, my dear. Just remember, if you want to see a change, you must, first, make a change.

During our conversation, Mrs. Holmes revealed portions of her youthful experiences.

Included was an account of the family's extreme indigence, that her mother had so much love to give, nobody realized the extent of lack. This beautiful matriarch concluded that she was the recipient of a great inheritance; her mother had no houses or land, but she gave her Jesus. Ultimately, that's all anybody needs.

Later, while reading selected passages, I found:

Seek ye first the Kingdom of Heaven and Its righteousness, and all other things shall be added.

And, as things began coming together, I read: In all thy ways, acknowledge me, and I shall direct thy path.

No, Cissy, I'm not preaching – just sharing (as you requested) with you how I found "peace, love, and happiness."

With my trust fund I bought this house. Six months after I met Mrs. Holmes, Joe and I repeated the nuptials. Prior to her visit, we were on the verge of going our separate ways.

Upon getting to know my fiancé, and in comparing him to other men I knew, I was elated over so many admirable traits and good looks that I grew dependent on him for survival. Without him, I felt doomed for failure.

In retrospect, Joe was smothered. His visits became more and more infrequent; and, if I didn't call, I wouldn't talk to him. Needless to say, I felt defeated.

For the first time in my life, I had fallen in love; and, it appeared that I had lost all hopes and dreams of paradise. When questioned, Joe maintained that he, too, was perplexed. But, I didn't believe him; it was he who had changed, not I.

I began dating other men, to my dismay. None were capable of meeting my expectations. Not understanding how or why, Joe and I got married. Gradually, I drifted back into being jealous, suspicious, possessive and accusatory. My husband was at his wit's end, and I was close to becoming an alcoholic.

Mrs. Holmes had left her telephone number with me; I used it. Immediately, she invited me over for "tea and talk."

"You're making a god of your husband, my dear," she chanted.

"That's a vast amount of pressure to put on the best – too much for the average."

Her words were, obviously, sincere; they hit me like a ton of bricks. Before we married, I had gone so far as to pray:

God, if You will just let me have Joe, I'll never ask for anything else.

Right after that prayer, Satan was in control of our relationship. It appeared that we could never rekindle what we once shared. Gradually, as I regained independence and redirected my priorities, Joe and I became closer. Now, we are spiritually bound, and communication is free.

Another destructive element of mine and Joe's relationship was my obsession to impress my "friends," associates, cohorts, and observers. Presently, I realize that I was, unduly, concerned about what others thought and said.

Cissy, I ask you, who shares my life (my bed, my bills, my love, my ups and downs – health, illnesses) – Joe, or my "friends?" More than you can ever imagine, this miraculous discovery and rechanneling process turned my world around.

***

When Russ and Lisa were fourteen and ten, respectively, Allen asked Connie for a divorce. Adamantly, she refused. Two weeks later, desperate for a listening ear, Connie called April January. April told her friend to wait thirty minutes and come over. Mrs. January did not have any brandy in the house. And, with Connie's state of hysteria, April knew they both would need it.

Sobbing madly, Connie's first words were almost inaudible.

"That bastard has taken my best years, given me two kids, built up his bank account, and shoved me aside like a worthless piece of junk. Now, he has the unmitigated gall to want a divorce."

Attempting to say and do all the right things to help, April sought to calm her companion, reminding Connie that things could be much worse. More than advice, Mrs. Stone wanted revenge: Mrs. January could only be a sounding board.

Connie began lamenting how the town's people would have more about which to talk. Another thought exploded!

"What man would want a ready-made family?"

April inquired about a projected settlement. Before she finished her remarks, Connie assured her friend that her spouse could not take what had never been his.

"Daddy bought that land, house and its furnishings; they're all mine. So, Allen knows better. He asked for half the savings, his personal things and one car."

As if struck by lightning, the soon-to-be dowager continued.

"It just dawned on me. If he's so willing to take that much of a loss, I could never raise my head anywhere within one hundred miles of Springfield. I can just hear the town's people, 'Stone must have really wanted to get rid of that bitch.'"

Mrs. January listened, attentively, as her friend released frustrations, anxieties, accusations and threats. April saw Connie's direction and wanted to assist in devising a scheme to make the latter happy, again. But, then, April thought: When has she ever been happy? Letting that rest, April began plotting.

Minutes later, the woman responded, simultaneously, to a noise in the hallway. Everything became very still, so they returned to their original positions.

As April was about to speak, the sound of an engine was heard. Looking at her watch, Mrs. January went to the door to peep out into her driveway. It was her son, Ronnie. Constance prepared to leave, but her diabolical mind said, "Share the idea with your hostess."

After Ronnie greeted their guest, he proceeded to retire to his room; he had a valedictory oration to deliver that night. In an attempt to sound rational and sincere, Connie's lips were contorted as she spoke.

"April, you are so lucky; you have a wonderful family, especially that Ronald. I know you're proud of him; of course, Catherine will be a heart breaker when she's older. But, what are Ronald's plans beyond high school graduation?"

Before her "accompanist" could respond, the beautiful aging representative of the bourgeois continued.

"I could arrange for him to secure a chauffeur's license; after all, I do need a driver. Sometimes, I drink a little too much at the club. In this day and time, Ronald would not claim this job as a life-long profession, but he could handle it, this summer. With college tuition increasing so, he can, probably, use as much financial assistance as possible."

Fearing her friend's reaction to be negative, without allowing rejection to be voiced at this point, Connie concluded.

"And, if college isn't his choice, working for Allen and me can expose him to other things. Do let me use the phone, April."

She paraded down the hall, and the trio of eavesdroppers scattered. They all ended up in the closet right by the telephone desk. The conversation was rather lengthy.

"Don't worry about asking him about it right away; I'm in no hurry. I've really got to be going, Darling, and thanks ever so much for being the friend you are."

With that, Constance Stone returned home in a different frame of mind.

When Allen came home about ten that night, Connie was sober and ingratiating, almost seductive. The suspecting husband inquired, "Is there a party scheduled?"

Book IV

STATE OF BEING

Several years later, and Ronald January has maintained the position as Chauffeur for the Stones, while attending evening school, working toward an Engineering degree.

He and Vance Brown were classmates and friends. Ronald informed his buddy that he would not be around for his group's debut, that he would be in California.

Lisa, Chris, Cissy, and Catherine were among the high school graduates. However, their main focal was the senior prom. Scheduled to perform for the occasion was the Brown Clan, the newest and hottest group in South Georgia.

Prior to prom time, the Browns had performed at various parties and social gatherings for several years, in nearby cities. The older sibling, Vance, being the business manager and spokesperson, had multiple meetings with Allen K. Stone. The bright youth had his eyes on recordings, tours, publicity, and all of the other normal goals of ambitious performers.

Vance had been trying to save the money he earned from the past four years of working two jobs. But, a few unexpected expenses had come up, and the other children were in school. Hence, there was one major obstacle blocking the aforementioned goals – no big money.

Stone was, seriously, considering acquiescing; he just needed time to negotiate a, mutually agreeable, contract. Vance was sharp enough to resist selling his soul in exchange for a favor. The aging attorney was not accustomed to dealing with "this new breed."

Allen had not heard the group, though invited time after time. But, he did know of their reputation as good kids, talented kids. His own offsprings had played in the school band with most of the Brown children. Stone decided to wait before making a final decision.

Anxious to please her brother, while giving in to a bit of curiosity, Lisa drove Blue to Chef Pizza. When they walked in, Russ was already there, hovering over a pitcher of beer, oblivious to the couple's arrival.

"Brother, dear, you look like the cat that swallowed the canary, and it didn't quite digest."

Rising and putting forth great effort to regroup, Russ said, "Sit down, you two, grab a glass and help me down this beer before it goes flat."

The couple sat down and, happily, followed through with Russ' request.

Minutes later.

"Russ, I've lived with you too long for games. What's wrong?"

The young man looked at his sister and then at his friend; the latter nodded in agreement with Lisa.

One of the main reasons Blue came home with me was to talk to Dad; also, we want to tape the music for prom night."

With her countenance registering confusion, Lisa interrupted.

"So, what's the crime? You've already talked to Dad, and the prom is tomorrow night; you haven't missed it!"

Russ signaled Lisa to cool it; Blue remained out of the family squabble.

"Lisa, just let me finish. Blue has had much experience in the recording business; he has good connections in California. In fact, that's where he was when he heard about the Brown Clan. Both of us will be job hunting in a couple of weeks, and we figured we'd talk to Dad about setting up a recording studio, serving the Browns, exclusively."

Lisa became bright-eyed with excitement.

"However," Russ continued, "there's been a slight change in plans."

This last statement made his friend's ears stand to attention. Barney, actually, felt a rush of warmth travel from his neck to his ears.

"Now, wait a minute, Russ; we discussed this very thoroughly before leaving State."

Remaining bewildered, Russ protested.

"Let me get to the point. Dad revealed his latest health problem."

He's dying – cancer – in the stomach; Larry Geiger has given him anywhere from six months to a year."

The big night, finally, arrived. The Brown Clan had gotten costumes designed (Thanks to Mrs. Brown) to compliment the class theme.

Earlier that morning, Lisa and a girlfriend had appointments at Springfield's most exclusive beauty salon. But, most of Lisa's excitement had diminished; she shared with her friend the fact that "something" had come up, at home, that left the family hurt. That was all the explanation Lisa could give right then: she was wrestling with reality, trying to map out what was happening to her young life.

As a child, mom was always around; as an adolescent, it was always Dad. And now, Mom is detached; Dad is dying.

Remembering last night's family dinner and the father-daughter chat, Lisa doubted that Connie even realized what was going on. Lisa felt sorry for her mother. For the past eight years, Connie had lived in a world all her own.

So, as her father said, "Tomorrow night is one of the biggest events in my baby's life; I don't want anything to interfere with her happiness. What's more, I'm releasing January to her disposal for the entire day. I won't accept anything but the best for you, Lisa. All the choices

I've made, whatever I've managed to acquire, it was all for my children. At this point, we will not talk about death or disease; we'll concentrate on life and health."

Lisa made no response; she and her father walked (hand-in-hand) down by the pool. And, for the second time in her life, she sought God for strength, courage, and determination.

Saturday morning, Lisa was awakened with a duet, coming in over the intercom on her wall. Not yet realizing her own identity, the girl was completely baffled as to recognizing this strange tune.

Suddenly, it stopped. Lisa drifted into a state of melancholy, debating return to sleep. Without warning, two lean figures burst into her room – one carrying a tray, smelling absolutely scrumptious – the other one was playing a guitar. Immediately, she sat up, yawning, "So this is the unrecognizable duet."

Russ and Blue were fighting to keep their promise to Allen K. Stone; today was considered all Lisa's.

Just as she finished brushing her teeth, another voice came over the intercom.

"Milady's car is ready; I understand the first stop is Jackie's – and on to the beauty parlor."

It was Ronnie January, their handsome chauffeur.

Though last night was a "bummer," Lisa had a smile. To the world, her father was a tyrant; to Lisa, Allen K. Stone was just an old softie.

About five, Sunday morning, a glowing young woman burst into her parent's bedroom. A king-sized bed set on a platform to the north; two peacock chairs were at the foot of the bed, facing a console that was located at the entrance of a balcony.

Near the bathroom (which houses an oval-shaped, walk-in tub) was a bronze fountain, surrounded by green plants. Connie had flown an architect in from the islands to design the hothouse that is adjoined to the balcony.

Before Lisa could say anything, her father propped himself up on his elbow and inquired.

"Honey, come sit here and tell your old man about the prom."

Allen pat the side of the bed, as he spoke.

"How was that band I've heard so much about?"

The girl was radiant as she confessed the professionalism of the Brown Clan. She filled her father in on every detail, including how Russ and Blue joined her and her date for breakfast. She did not reveal how uncomfortable she felt in Blue's presence.

Though Allen was concerned about her activities, he led his daughter back to a thorough rendition of the band's overall performance.

At six-thirty, Constance Stone had had all she could take of this incessant chatter; she scurried off to her hot house and retired, as was customary. Ignoring his wife's abrupt departure, Allen continued questioning Lisa, whom he trusted greatly.

By seven-thirty, Allen and his daughter had settled in the kitchen, drinking coffee. He decided to level with Lisa and inform her of Vance's proposition, that after her description and excitement, Allen K. Stone was willing to go out that evening to witness their potential rehearsal.

Having forgotten the black cloud of a terminal disease, Stone telephoned his business manager to request the necessary papers to be prepared, also, to inform him that he was expected to be there.

Lisa was beside herself with excitement, not remembering that she remained sleepless.

After the telephone conversation, Stone suggested that they both get some rest. With four years of deliberation under his belt, Allen K. Stone consented to become procurator of the Brown Clan, by nightfall.

At noon, Connie stumbled into the kitchen and ran up on Barney Blue.

"Why, good morn-er-afternoon, Mrs. Stone. Did you rest well?"

Blue was having coffee and offered to pour his gracious hostess a cup.

"Thanks, Barney, but, where's Amanda? She was supposed to have my protein drink ready."

The young man shrugged his shoulders and continued getting the coffee ready. She wore a wig, this morning. He was sure, now. She was the mystery woman in California!

She sat down, perpetually inquiring, "Where's Russ? Is he still asleep? You know, it's so strange – when my children were younger, they and I were inseparable. But, now all they need is their father."

"What do you think about my becoming a talk show hostess?"

Connie looked drained and said as she began reminiscing over the earlier years and suggesting challenging projects.

Charmingly, Blue tolerated the revelations; neither mentioned their previous encounter.

Upstairs, Russ was in the shower; his sister knocked at his door. After waiting for his usual "Yeah – come," Lisa entered, heard the shower and sat on his bed to wait.

Minutes later, Russ emerged from the bathroom, shocked to see his sister.

"Now, who's looking like the cat that swallowed the canary?"

Russ was drying his hair with a towel. Waiting for Lisa to declare reason for her presence, he joined his sister on the bed.

"Russ, you'll never guess what happened! This morning, Dad phoned Marvin and told him about the Brown Clan. By this evening, they'll be on their way. Knowing Marvin, he has already run up a phone bill, tracking down engagements.

Russ could hardly believe his ears! Forgetting about his wet hair, he began questioning his sister about her information.

His final query, "Where's Blue? He'll flip out over this. I can't believe it, and here I was thinking that all hope was lost, but Lisa, what about his condition?"

As though the "condition" didn't exist, the young woman had begun to relate to her father as always. Expressionless, Lisa thought: Why did Russ have to burst my bubble?

"Russ, Dad feels that the most important thing is for us to help him live life to its fullest, until he's no longer able. So, let's not talk about it; we have a full day ahead of us."

A very sleepy Vance Brown was aroused by the telephone. At first, he was annoyed to be awakened, but when he discovered the nature of the call, he leapt across the room, putting on robe and thongs, simultaneously.

He got everybody else up; they all joined him in the den to hear the news.

"But," Vance continued, "We're in a better situation; Russ, Lisa and their friend, Blue, are on our side."

Corneilius and Mary were just as overjoyed as their children; they had always been a source of inspiration, support, and strength for the household.

Corneilius and Mary were, traditionally, a loving and devoted couple. As head of the family, Corneilius had more than lived up to his expectations; as wife, mother, friend, and companion, Mary surpassed any other. Each had always attended church, regularly. But, more than that, the couple taught their children independence, care and concern, respect for Inner Power, dignity, and gratitude, from the beginning.

They believed that "children live what they learn." Though neither participated in marching, demonstrating, the sit-ins, the stand-ins, etc., the Browns, adamantly, believed and taught that, "All men are created equal."

Mr. Brown was always quiet, but watchful; his forte was to know when to speak. Though he lacked college training, Corneilius finished high school, with honors. Few people knew this. He, seldom, talked about the past, except to show parallels or patterns.

This self-made man was forever striving, quietly, to pave the way for his children and other people to have a better tomorrow, in spite of the inequality among races.

When Corneilius heard of his children's good fortune, he remembered the eloquent words for President Kennedy, delivered on June 11, 1963:

We are confronted primarily with a moral issue. It is as old as the Scriptures and is as clear as the American Constitution. One hundred years of delay have passed since President Lincoln freed the slaves, yet their heirs, their grandsons, are not fully free. They are not yet freed from the bonds of injustice. They are not yet

freed from social and economic oppression. And this nation for all its hopes and its boasts, will not be fully free until all its citizens are free... Now the time has come for this nation to fulfill its promise.

Not considered an overly religious man among members of the cloth, his peers and family thought him to be the epitome of spiritual wealth.

Because he did not accept a position on the deaconic staff, Corneilius Brown was black-balled as a man of God among members of the neighborhood Black Baptist Church. They could not understand how a person could profess Christianity and turn down the opportunity to serve. However, the senior Brown maintained that he did not have any objections to organized religion, if it followed through with its proclaimed purpose. To him, this appointment was, politically, motivated.

Too often, he found people holding positions for social rank.

Too often, he discovered the existence of idol gods being worshipped, taking the form of anything from money to people, from anger to hate. Too often, he had seen intellects function without the Spirit part (the God business), thinking, "We will do it all with our heads; we are smart."

As a child, Corneilius remembered how much confusion he and the other children suffered, how they thought God just watched you all day long to "catch" you. That He would, then, just punish or reward you, accordingly.

But, this man was determined that his children would have a clearer understanding of how God is a Spirit which is housed in every soul – there to lead, not trap.

Mr. Brown would, dutifully, accompany his wife and children to Sunday School and Church, at least twice a month. He worked two jobs, and it was difficult to always be "Johnny-on-the-spot."

Daily, his children witnessed this determined specimen rise and assume his responsibility with a quiet dignity, remaining open-minded and always willing to listen to a suggestion.

He, just, did not see the need to seek public approval, not even from the church, for his decisions. Seldom would Corneilius change his mind, but he would weigh another opinion. If it made sense and he could weigh more advantages by changing, he would. He believed that a person would reap as he has sown.

On the other hand, the Brown children were exposed to a mother who saw no wrong or bad in anyone. When an accused person was void of an excuse, Mary would provide one. Though she shared the concept of "Spirit" with her husband, she maintained that people would do better if they knew better.

Perhaps that's a main reason as to why this optimistic woman considered it a pleasure to raise her children as well as her younger sister (a menopause baby), and a friend's daughter. Mrs. Brown believed that every experience, good or bad, served as a catalyst for growth. And, her compassion, patience, love, and understanding surpassed most.

Realizing that "trouble is, sometimes, opportunity," Mary seldom panicked during a family crisis; she taught prayer and meditation as the only means to solving a problem.

She, frequently, quoted, "…weeping may tarry for the night, but joy comes with the morning."

Another favorite was, "In everything, God works for good with those who love Him, who are called according to His purpose."

Mary Lou Brown, truly, felt that trouble was the other side of blessings.

Corneilius and Mary taught their children to feel good about themselves, because everybody was made by God, that each person has a special reason for being alive. Most of the siblings exhibited level-headedness, especially the oldest, Vance.

After the meeting was over that Sunday evening, Corneilius treated the entire family to fountain treats at the town's only Black-owned soda shop.

Later at nightfall, seated in the den, the Brown family continued in the spirit of celebration, but they all knew that this new endeavor involved much serious soul-searching and planning.

"This is a big responsibility; we're no longer talking chump change, juke joints, and holes-in-the walls. Our habits need modifying; our time will have to be better utilized, which means more practice and less socializing. But, we don't want to be all fagged out at thirty, so we must schedule proper rest and diet. Right, Mama?"

They all laughed as their parents gestured approval.

Vance continued.

"And, as for you little squirts, I yield the floor to Daddy, 'cause I know he has something to say about school and homework."

It was three a.m. when they went to bed.

When fall came, Corneilius, proudly, got in touch with the principals involved, as well as each homeroom teacher. They agreed to a liberal attendance schedule, as long as grades were maintained.

However, if anybody's average began declining, a tutor would have to be hired. Corneilius added the latter. He knew that it would take both Brain <u>and</u> Green Power for true success.

Everybody was popular and well-liked in school, so the children had no problem in locating a willing friend to keep "good notes."

***

In a way, you have to allow your man to be the head, while you act as neck, thereby, turning the head with love, tenderness, understanding and concern. "Behind every good man (though, sometimes, ahead) is a good woman."

Cissy, the last time I was home, Mary told you that a person is treading dangerous ground when one begins to use sex as a weapon. You know better than I as to why she made that statement. And, believe me, I am not qualified to judge. But, I do remember that you told me whenever you wanted to have your way, you would put your husband on a "sex diet."

***

Among the many elated people in Springfield, Cathi was, by far, the most. She and Vance had been dating for three years. Vance Brown thought himself especially lucky to have a girl like Catherine January at his every beck and call.

She was short, thin, somewhat aggressive, yet charming and shy. Everybody said "yes" to Cathi without measuring the odds. When met with opposition, she schemed until gaining victory. "….victory over the grave…"

After Allen K. Stone began to play a different role in the Brown's lives, they began to prosper, overnight. Of course, Barney Blue was one of the main boosters behind this small town success story. Russ and Lisa, too, shared in the glory. But, to Stone's dismay, Blue would, and justifiably so, receive credit for the longest bar on a graph that measured individual contributions.

Catherine's girlfriends began to plant ideas in her head about other women taking Betty Wright's "Clean-up Woman," that she had invested too much time in "that fish" to let him get away.

"Now, you know that this is war, and in war, women have to use their best weapons, their gold mines..."

"Girl, you must be crazy, you'd better get that dude – making money, good looking..."

Admittedly, Cathi had been thinking along the same lines. However, Vance had never mentioned marriage; he was not seeing anybody else – he would not even consider that. But, he had a goal to attain. He always, assumed that one day, he and Cathi might marry, but Vance just did not ponder the subject.

"Honey, when will your family's schedule be flexible enough for us to spend a weekend someplace?"

Vance held his girl in his arms as they sat staring at the huge screen, at a drive-in, three miles out of town.

"Cathi, you're so sweet, and you've been very patient during my recent transition. I don't know, Babe; everything is topsy turvy, right now. Just give me a while; I'll look over the schedule with Blue and give you a call. O.K.?"

Judging from his tone of voice and her years of experience, Cathi knew what she had just received permission to do. Conveniently, this beautiful "Jezebel," who could put Michaelangelo to shame, left her contraceptive home. Since her conversation with the girls, Catherine January decided to discard her pills and buy some "foam."

Rockets were launched, bells rang, and angels descended – Vance had just finished making love to his soon-to-be-bride, an activity in which she, readily, engaged.

The first time Vance made love to Cathi, he thought her to be a virgin. Though he never found out, Catherine began to experiment with sex at a very young age.

During one of her eavesdropping sessions with her friends, Cathi overheard her mother and Constance Stone declare that by douching with allum, a girl could reinstate her virginity.

When Cathi met Vance, he thought her to be sweet and innocent. In keeping with her role, she had to be untouched; so, she got with her friends and drove off to find Fletcher, the gas station attendant. If anybody had contacts, Fletcher did. Also, his mother was a renowned believer in roots and herbs.

When the magic moment arrived, Vance was nervous; he didn't want to hurt his girl.

They had dated six months before indulging in heavy petting. (Meanwhile, Catherine was involved in four affairs).

Her skin was smooth and smelled so sweet that Vance could hardly contain himself. He had promised to "take it slow and easy." They were in the central part of "The Path," so as to detect approaching vehicles from either side.

Catherine had worn a blue jean skirt so that it wouldn't look wrinkled, when she got home. Also, she knew that Vance should have easier access to her charms. He brought along a fifth of wine, at Cathi's request. She drank almost all of it. Clumsily, yet cautiously,

Vance removed Cathi's clothing and proceeded to unite their bodies, which made him feel like a little boy on Christmas morning.

Afterwards, this skillful Madonna laid her head on his chest and sobbed. Taking the cue, Vance held his love in silence.

Book V

THE EMERGENCE

The phone rang, and quite by accident, Vance answered. It was Catherine; she sounded terrified of something, and this realization jolted the talented musician to life.

"I just can't say too much over the phone, honey; I'll be waiting."

The phone went dead.

"I've practiced this moment a million times in the mirror, and now that you're here, I'm at a loss for words."

"Babe, just come right out and tell me; whatever it is, it can't be that bad."

Cathi played the role to a tee, as she led him onto the back porch.

"I missed a period. Last week, I fainted while I was doing the dishes. Luckily, Cissy was the one who found me; I got her to promise not to tell anybody by swearing to see about myself that evening. The doctor confirmed pregnancy."

Vance was, absolutely, stunned! For a while, he was speechless.

However, after a moment of regrouping, in his characteristic fashion, the young man soothed his betrothed.

On his way home, Vance thought: What kind of blessing is this? How do I tell Mama?

In keeping with tradition, Mary met this problem, courageously.

"Well, darling, at least you're a bread winner, now. Things could be worse; this may have occurred before Mr. Stone came into our lives. Cathi seems like a nice enough girl; she'll,

probably, make a good wife."

As Mary spoke these words, she felt a bit uneasy. Though she taught her boys to be careful, to face life responsibly, she could not help but to recall various innuendoes Cissy had made about Catherine.

Dutifully, the wedding was planned and executed, a lovely and elaborate affair.

When they were, finally, left alone, Cathi lit a cigarette; obviously adjusted to its effect, she sighed and relaxed.

Shocked, yet unassuming, Vance inquired, "Babe, since when did you start smoking?"

Before now, Vance had never seen his bride smoke; since he detested cigarettes, Cathi had not revealed her habit of several years. After all, she couldn't allow anything to ruin her plans.

The smoking surprise was one among many. Vance discovered several other things the night their twins were born. Cathi had just been brought into her room, which was a private one.

She had secured services from the best team of obstetricians, located fifteen miles from Springfield. Consequently, the hospital was rated as "too expensive" for most.

The Brown family's life-style had changed with moderation, until Cathi joined the household.

When Vance came home with builders to construct a swimming pool, Mary knew her son's heart was like a time-bomb – waiting, just waiting.

Though they all liked nice things, the family had, formerly, made a truce – to discuss any changes before acting on it. Vance had been the one to suggest it; everybody figured him to be the last to break it.

Tiptoeing into his wife's room, with a grin from ear-to-ear, carrying a bouquet of red roses behind his back, Vance peeped in at Cathi.

She was not sleep; in fact, she was cursing and tugging at her gown.

"These damn stitches – nobody ever told me I'd hurt like this! This is it, man, no more babies; I'm back on the pills, Van."

He had never heard her curse before.

Bewildered, disgruntled, disgusted, yet in love, this pioneering spirit was true to form.

"Oh, Babe, you just feel a little sore, right now. Calm down; look at these roses – they're fresh, too."

By this time, Mary had arrived to congratulate her son and daughter-in-law, and to greet her first grands.

"Mrs. Brown, how long will I hurt like this?"

Mary smiled and said, "Don't worry, Sweetheart; you'll be able to tell a difference by tomorrow."

Before she could inquire about her grandchildren, Cathi groaned and asked her husband for assistance to the bathroom.

Friend after friend, and relative after relative – each scampered in to see the twins, bring gifts, and extend congratulations.

The media had gotten wind of the new arrivals, and fans responded. When Catherine left the hospital, her gifts and flowers filled four vans.

At home, Cathi insisted on having a nurse in attendance. Vance protested, initially, but, after a while, they compromised. Instead of six weeks, the nurse was hired for seven days. After all, two babies with healing navels and circumcisions needed "professional care."

Instantly, Catherine discovered another means of manipulation – the twins.

Though both grandparents were available, to say nothing of relatives and friends, Cathi required a nurse trained in pediatrics. When her friends visited, they were, fairly so, impressed and expressive.

The twins were six months old before Cathi allowed Vance to touch her, again. Being on the road so much, he had not noticed anything different.

True to her words, Cathi started taking the "pill," again.

After being on the road six straight weeks, Vance crawled in bed dead tired, but needing his beautiful wife. Instead, she lectured him on the hard role of a housewife and mother of two.

On a tour in Jamaica, Vance met a shy and attractive girl, whose sincerity and capacity for loving scared him.

The twins were almost two years old, and since their birth, Cathi had made love to her husband three times. He was starved, for more than he realized.

The former Miss January had never loved herself; thereby not being capable of loving anyone else.

Catherine found out about this tete-a-tete and became enraged. Scurrying off to Cissy's, she took time to select the perfect outfit and freshen her make-up.

Cissy's first marriage took place three days after high school graduation. She was seventeen and pregnant. He was eighteen and in love with himself.

After four months, she lost the baby, and their already deteriorating relationship exploded, permanently. He was never home, and she sat around crying all day and feeling sorry for herself.

One weekend, before the break-up, the young couple was favored with his relatives

spending some time with them. Amid the entourage was a rich play uncle from Detroit. He was thirty-three years old, divorced and had two children. His worldly mannerisms swept Cissy off her feet.

The family went out for dinner, except Cissy and Uncle James. Cissy was nauseous and Uncle consented to staying behind, thereby being company for the ailing mother-to-be.

"Come here, Baby, lie down and put your head in Unc's lap."

Like an obedient child, Cissy lay on the couch and placed her head in James' lap. She felt pampered, loved, and appreciated.

Expressed emotions were void in her life, especially with Raymond, her young husband. He felt trapped into a marriage.

After the miscarriage, per request, Cissy flew to Detroit. James was waiting for her at the airport with a dozen long stem roses and three barrels of charm. He dined and wined her sufficiently.

Meanwhile, Uncle James set the wheels in motion for Cissy's freedom.

"What shall we do tonight to celebrate your freedom, Sweet One?"

"I'm not really in the mood for going out, James, let me cook dinner for us."

"Nothing doing; you're too precious to sweat over a hot stove. Grab a magazine, put your feet up, and I'll order Chinese Cuisine."

After dinner, James coerced Cissy to have her fill of coke, reefer, and wine.

The next morning she awoke to find herself wrapped in the arms of her new found lover and friend. They left for a week in Nassau and three days in Jamaica.

Cissy had never known such happiness. She, readily, consented to marry James. And, she knew that she would never return to small town thrills.

Nine months later, Cissy overheard a conversation between James and his first wife. She thought it was a dream; so, she ignored what she heard and continued to be happy.

Then, without warning, James became upset over nothing. Everything said made matters worse. He began beating her until she could stand it no longer.

"Mary, I want to come home."

"Of course, Cissy, we'll talk when you get here, if you feel up to it. Do you have money for plane fare?"

Cissy never confided in her sister; she just grew bitter with resentment and envy.

After sharing her dilemma with her friend, Cathi realized what she must do; she flushed her remaining pills down the toilet.

Two weeks later, when Vance arrived home from a festival, Catherine was wearing a silk gown that he had never seen. Caught completely off guard, the accomplished musician inquired, "What's this all about?"

With her usual charm and beauty, Cathi had her husband right where she wanted him.

Two months later, while at family dinner, the announcement was made.

In her fifth month of pregnancy, Catherine began complaining of lower back pain.

Again, Vance was sent to the arms of his Jamaican princess, who never questioned the length of time between their meetings.

Though his wife knew about the affair, she never mentioned it. After all, she was his wife; their marriage license meant he wasn't free to entertain any thoughts of "that other woman as anything but his whore; besides, all men sow their wild oats."

So, Cathi resigned herself to relieving Van of as much money as possible.

That way, "the Jamaica bitch can't even rank as his mistress. If he thinks he can leave me, I'll take everything he can ever hope to have."

After their third son was born and Catherine was up and about, Vance asked for a divorce. When Cathi finished voicing her threats, her husband gave her a cheerful reminder that the house they shared belonged to his parents.

Wisely, Vance had not purchased a home for his family; he kept waiting for his marriage to improve. He and the twins were inseparable and two of the only things he had in common with his wife.

Finally, Vance and his father had a talk.

"Son, I've found that you have to seek God's guidance in everything you do."

Van knew he had not sought Divine Guidance before he married Catherine; so, he was a bit hesitant, now, though he knew there was no other way.

Corneilius further stated, "Sometimes, men don't always go after the right things in a woman. Too often, we are blinded by their charm and tricks. Unfortunately, there are no courses that teach common sense and good judgment. I was blessed to find Mary; she's always been a light in my life. We got married young, too; but, we were lucky, I suppose. I think I'll run for a seat on the school board.

Somebody needs to get classes started in reality approaches to living. We do all the right things for the wrong reasons."

Vance got the message: That's your problem; you solve it. Mine and your mama's love go with you always.

Rumor had it that Barney Blue and Cathi were lovers, that she was the instigator. These accusations were whispered among certain groups; it never became public knowledge.

When the baby boy was two years old, Vance visited Jamaica to find his believe engaged. The weeding was two days off.

For the first time since they met, each acknowledged the love that had grown for the other. (That's the thing about genuine love, you don't "fall" into it; you "grow" into it).

Torn between emotions and reality, Vance gave in to the latter. He wished his love eternal happiness and bade her farewell.

Returning home, Van pleaded with Cathi, "Babe, we've lost whatever we had; there's no other woman – I just want out. Take whatever you want, do what you have to, just leave."

Sullenly, the wife inquired, "And, what about the children? I suppose you think I'll give them to you. There's no way any court in Georgia would give wandering father custody of three young boys."

In a way, she was right. He could go the "unfit mother" route, but Van wanted to avoid a scandal. Cathi didn't care one way or another. Whatever happened, she would never work; that was her only true concern.

Book VI

PREPARING FOR THE HARVEST

Peace Is Promised

There is a famine in this land,
In past lay heavily In my soul,
Whose footprints tread upon the sand
Of those without a common goal.

There's a purpose for every life,
Each distinct within its own right,
Reaching upward, conquering strife,
If being influenced by eternal Light.

One's need for sight is opportunity,
Not each step – nor even the way,
Let open the door of Faith and unity,
Three and you control each day.

Truth abounds as shepherd and sheep –
Awaiting entrance to mankind's souls,
Approaching in the still, it creeps
With choices that prayer unfolds.

Possession – revelation, they carry a price
So oft discovered too late;
While fate denounces our vice,
Peace and Love are at the gate.

Catherine was driving home; the boys were playing hide and seek in the Benz station wagon.

While visiting, this desperate young woman had consumed too much alcohol. Mrs. Stone was there, and they all drank brandy until Mrs. January called "cease fire."

As April was getting more ice and making a phone call for her husband, Constance shared her scheme with Catherine.

The older woman had been making tapes of Allen's every contact. The phones were bugged (at the offices as well as home); she had even planted one under the driver's seat in the limousine.

Also, Ronald would report Stone's schedules, plans, and meetings. Connie wanted to ruin Allen, completely. Over a period of years, she had collected over a thousand tapes.

Though Ronnie was her brother, Cathi admired Mrs. Stone for being so clever. The girl knew her brother had been "making it" with Constance, but she didn't know to what extent.

Influenced by what Connie shared, Cathi began devising plans of her own. At the moment she placed the last piece of her puzzle, the car began skidding. As rare as it was, snow and ice was on the ground.

A police care and ambulance sped toward Cathi at a light.

Between the noise the boys were making, the radio, her condition, and her thoughts, she did not hear or see the approaching vehicles.

Catherine got her wish: She never worked; Van lost his boys.

Heartbroken and filled with despair, Vance went to see Allen K. Stone. It was three days after the burials, and the weather remained cold. When he arrived, Van was stunned to see the old man looking so puny. Stone had lost weight all over, even in his face.

Ignorant of his disease, the young man inquired, "Been on a diet, Mr. Stone?"

The aging gentleman accepted that excuse and changed the subject.

"You're still a young man, Van; don't throw your life away. It looks dark now, but everything will get brighter, in time."

Not having heard Stone articulate any signs of faith, in the past. Vance knew all was not well. As his mother, highly, recommended, "If you think your grass is dying, walk in your neighbor's yard."

After Allen's last comment, Van offered to treat his host at a nearby, quiet bar. It was time for true confession.

When they neared the end of the driveway, Vance spotted smoke coming from the Stones' bedroom.

In a drunken stupor, Constance had knocked over a chemistry set in the hot house. Attempting to clean up the mess, she dropped her cigarette, and, in fifteen minutes, the area was engulfed with flames. She lost her sense of direction and got trapped. Though the fire department salvaged most of the house, Constance Stone died, instantly.

That same night, Allen suffered an acute attack of stomach pain. He was hospitalized and was not able to attend the funeral.

·Gradually, Allen became a vegetable, and his children were forced to put him in Lady Immaculate.

Corneilius and Mary Brown would, frequently, have Russ and Lisa Stone over, especially for Sunday dinner. Barney Blue stayed out of town more than the others; however, he was welcomed whenever his schedule permitted, especially by Lisa.

Though extremely difficult and trying, nine months after such a stream of tragedy,

Mary noticed that her son was looking better. Vance found his world to be of strange pickings,

yet he knew all that had happened was the result of choices and decisions.

With this outlook, Vance and Mary were, highly, instrumental in helping the Stone children accept their fate. After a while, they all become one big, happy family.

Both Marvin and Amanda remained in the employ of their new bosses: Russ, Lisa and Barney. Their chauffeur, Ronnie January, thought it wise to pursue the career for which he was trained. The money he had saved over the years enabled him to go into business for himself.

Marvin's crush had widened for Amanda; she returned his affection, and Lisa's urging led them to the altar. More and more, love seemed to move in where once resided hate.

Amanda was frying peach pies, a household favorite, as Lisa, casually, strolled in and tickled the woman's neck with a piece of paper. Affectionately, the housekeeper tapped the girl on her hand.

"What are you up to, now? Have you, at last, found a man who meets your approval?"

Each question Amanda asked was met with a devilish smile and a headshake. Finally, Lisa produced a deed declaring Marvin and Amanda owners of a piece of land, as well as an agreement from Ace Construction Company, to build a house of their choice.

Both were permanent fixtures at the Stone house, and they knew that. But, Russ, Lisa and Barney wanted the couple to have their own little "piece of the rock."

Disappointed and a bit disillusioned, Vance discovered his Jamaican princess remarried. A year after the tragedies, he made a long distance telephone call. A small, sweet voice whispered, "Hello."

Van proceeded to inquire about her marriage, which ended in divorce two years after exchanging wedding vows. However, the young man's excitement was short-lived.

Maria informed her suitor that she thought his relationship to be reconciled, and had remarried, just one week before his call.

Vance Brown, a lonely but loving man, became more of a "workaholic" than before. Conveniently, business was demanding; so, there was no problem in locating something to do.

Could this recent turn of events be an indication that Cathi had powers that proclaimed victory over the grave? Was this season due him?

***

According to your recollection of the meeting between Patrick and Mary, all went well. Did your sister say something, afterwards, intimating Mr. Donovan to be a scoundrel? Or, is the thing about his lacking a sense of humor the only problem?

Regardless, Cissy, you have to make your own decisions; after all, you're the one who has to live with the consequences.

After I got to know Joe, the thought never entered my mind to get a second opinion. There were definite and positive vibes that I recognized to be undisputed.

Mary, constantly, advised us not to worry about knowing when true love is present; somehow, you're made aware.

***

Indeed Mary Brown can be considered a good person to have in your corner. While Larry Geiger remained baffled as to Allen Stone's longevity, Mary assured Lisa.

"God can be God all by Himself. It is Divine Love and will power that's keeping your father alive."

Lisa understood her father to possess tremendous drive, and she knew it was for her, most times.

"Ultimately, love triumphs, which is what God represents. Doctors and nurses are very skillful, most certainly, needed; but, they can only give their knowledge. The layman can only give love; frequently, that's all he has."

"But, Mary, how can you let go of someone you love, when that time does come?"

"Sometimes, Lisa, the greatest act of love is demonstrated by letting go."

With much to deliberate, Lisa Stone reached her hand into the cookie jar for the third time.

"I don't know; I, just, don't know."

Sensing the girl's thirst, Mary went to the refrigerator for milk. She poured two glasses, one for herself, as well. It was like the old days, Mary choosing the kitchen for her private "pow wows."

Downstairs, in the music room, the Brown Clan rehearsed as the ladies prepared refreshments. Corneilius was enjoying his riding mower, as well as listening to his children practice. The music seemed to inspire Mr. Brown, and before he realized it, the front and back yards were trimmed, perfectly.

As he cut the lawn and worked in the flower garden, Corneilius reminisced the Black man's struggle, as studied, heard, and witnessed – how most proved capable of productivity.

That's another reason he was proud of this children. One day, each would be, financially, independent, having produced a socially and universally accepted commodity.

When he "was coming along," not many of his peers were, overly, ambitious. They figured, "What's the use?" There were others who protested racial discrimination, physically as well as emotionally.

Corneilius recalled how "bent out of shape" his pal, Rap, got in 1963, when four Black girls were bombed in Birmingham, during Sunday School, after demonstrations were held there. Though everybody was hurt and upset, Rap was the most enraged and vengeful.

This was a memorable year; Medgar Evers was, also, killed. However, Blacks made a tremendous step toward unity in 1963, when participating in "The March on Washington."

And, Dr. Martin Luther King shared a dream for his people:

I have a dream that one day, on the red hills of Georgia, sons of former slaves and the sons of former slave owners will be able to sit down together at the table of brotherhood.
I have a dream that one day even the State of Mississippi, a state sweltering with the heat of injustice, sweltering with the heat of oppression, will be transformed into an oasis of freedom and justice.
I have a dream that my little children will one day live in a nation where they will not be judged by the color of their skin but by the content of their character.

By 1964, violence remained on the south's surface. In Mississippi, thirty Black churches
were either bombed or lay victim to arson.

"Yet," Mr. Brown sighed, "We survived, and in certain corners lay semblance of change."
Then, he thought about people like Fletcher, who refused to exercise his right to vote. So many people shed blood and died for that opportunity.

Corneilius put his lawn mower up. As he was locking the utility room, he overheard Russell Stone and Barney Blue discussing library and park construction, plans for a piece of property, east of Marvin's lot.

With a disgusting sigh, Mr. Brown sat down. What he remembered, at that point, was witnessed by his paternal grandfather:

In 1898, a Contract of Sales was written declaring that Ike Liberty purchased two separate pieces of land, though the original deed wasn't delivered until 1907.

One lot consisted of fifty-eight acres, while the other one measured fifty-six. Mr. Liberty passed the property down to His two sons, Ike, Jr., and Francis. Ike, Jr., had two daughters (Chris' grandmother and her sister). Francis had several children.

Ike, Jr., died when his children were fairly young; consequently, his brother raised the girls, who were legal heirs to half the property. However, being minors, Francis was in control of all the property.

With racial injustice being what it was, both girls fled the south to New York, as soon as they became of age.

Francis could only utilize so much of the property at one time; so, he deemed it unnecessary to stand watch over the unused acreage.

Meanwhile, Allen K. Stone's father-in-law began growing crops on several acres of the unattended land. But, before planting, the elderly gentleman cut down the timber and sold it.

After Constance and Allen married, the latter was informed about the crops.

"How many years has this been going on?"

"Well, Son, as near as I can tell, I'd say about eighteen years."

"Guessing isn't good enough. Don't you have something with a date on it?"

Stone made such an issue of the date that his father-in-law began rambling through his old records. Puzzled, the old man questioned his new son-in-law.

"What's so all-fired important about the date, Allen?"

Finally, it was produced. Stone breathed relief, "Two more years and the Liberty family will be relieved."

The old man grew weary of asking, so he dismissed the issue.

Before his death, two years after the discussion, Stone and Constance were declared heirs to his estate.

Five years passed, and Francis Liberty decided to sell one hundred acres and retain fourteen. When this announcement reached Allen, he made several phone calls. Later that afternoon, Francis appeared at the office of Allen K. Stone.

Though angry and embittered, the Black man knew to "walk softly" until the matter could be settled in court. Stone's explanation was like a foreign language – "...party of the part..."

Three months later, the judge ruled Allen K. Stone legal owner of fifty acres of property, which was, originally, owned by Ike Liberty, Sr. The presiding magistrate explained it all to Francis.

"You see, Son, it is like this, the law states that if any person (with the original owner's consent) lives on, or uses, a

parcel of land for twenty-one years, consecutively, he owns it. This Ordinance is called 'Adverse Possession'."

Rising and shaking off ghosts of the past, Corneilius joined his family in the music room. He thought: Russ doesn't seem like he has the blood of injustice flowing in his veins. But, then, neither does Blue exemplify traits of subservience as did many Blacks in the past.

Mary and Lisa descended the stairs with enough snacks and refreshments for everybody. They spent the entire day together.

Russ was tired, but Barney and Lisa wanted to go riding. They rode near "The Path." Pointing, Lisa smiled and said, "Barney, that property right over there has been the topic of many conversations. If trees could talk."

Both laughed, agreeably.

"But," the girl continued, "with time, comes change. In a few years, that same spot will be a public library. The Browns are donating a music collection."

Blue recognized the old black Cadillac straight ahead; it was Fletcher's. He had been Barney's contact for purchasing marijuana. Judging from movement and sound, the passengers assumed somebody must have been enjoying nature.

"Lisa, how do you manage? Most girls are out trapping guys. But, you hang under Russ and me all the time."

"Good observation, Pal; what about you guys? Every female I know is freaking out over one or the other of you –for what, I don't know."

Again, the couple shared a hearty laugh.

After her initial case of nervousness, Lisa and Barney had developed a friendship that was as strong as hers and Russell's. They drove until midnight. Russ was asleep long before the car pulled into the garage. Barney retired to his room and Lisa to hers. Both dreamed of holding each other.

The following Monday, the young Miss Stone rode into town with Russ and Barney, teasing her brother about the mayor's daughter, an old romance.

"When Marvin and Amanda move into their new home, I'm moving, too," the Californian revealed.

"Like hell you will" exclaimed Russ!

Lisa felt a cold chill run down her back; goose pimples rose on her arms.

"Barney, why on earth would you do something so drastic?"

"Hold on. Give me a chance to explain; I believe you'll see things my way. This is a small town. Neither of your parents resides with you guys anymore, and I'm a single – Black man."

Both of the Stones protested, but Blue stood his ground. In fact, he and Fletcher had already discussed the possibility of sharing a three story house on Cottage Drive. When this was stated, Lisa exploded!

Though Russ objected, he voiced no further questions or comments. Blue pleaded his case; he felt like he needed Lisa's approval.

After spending the day philosophizing and reasoning, a compromise was reached: Blue would, at least, look around for another roommate.

That night, Lisa awakened from a dream, realizing the solution for the household's existing problem.

***

So far, Cissy, this letter has pictured Joe as recipient of all the glory; me, as the sinner. However, I wanted to "fess" up, first. One thing I've learned, nothing is ever resolved by shifting the blame. Many people can see others' faults, but not their own. I would love to be able to take credit for all the sense; unfortunately, I can't even imagine it.

Remember how we use to respond to our chronic name callers, "It takes one to know one." Though spoken matter-of-factly, that statement carries a lot of weight. Unless you're doing a certain thing yourself, why else would you be suspicious or accusatory of someone else?

Last Saturday, Joe served me "brunch" in bed. It was about 11:00. (Saturdays bring out the laziness in me). He, frequently, volunteers pleasantries, though he was hung up on role-playing, initially, - who the chef was, in particular.

We had been married about four months (At that time, I was working out of the office. Joe got home before I did). We greeted each other with a kiss; afterwards, I went straight to bed. He thought I was changing clothes. Realizing how long I'd been gone, my husband, very sweetly, asked, "Is the cook on strike, tonight?"

A slap in the face couldn't have hurt more. I reminded him that both of us were working an eight hour day. And, one thing led to another. Joe ended the discussion; he thought I was angry because of how I emphasized certain words.

"Tell you what, let's go out to dinner."

"Fine, Joe, but that's a short-term solution; what about tomorrow?"

I swear, friend, Joe has the temperament needed in politics; I've, rarely, seen him over react to anything.

***

Politics drew little attention around the Brown household, other than being exposed enough to make decent judgments on election days. Then, one day, Patrick Donovan surfaced. Suddenly, "old glories" were everywhere; hats, banners, buttons, etc., were interspersed over the music room floor.

Cissy Coan had made a pop call on her sister. Blushing and talking one hundred MPH, Cissy told the family about this nice, young politician "whose honesty is astounding for his profession."

Patrick Donovan's father had been one of the first Black policemen in Atlanta. He was hired at a time when Black cops could only arrest Black violators, among those who had to change into their uniforms at the YMCA.

The young man was reared by parents who insisted that he become educated, and learn protocol, as well.

His mother taught at an all-Black high school. Patrick was an only child. Even in elementary school, the lad was popular among teenagers. He, frequently, stayed with his mother until she was off. His school let out at 2; hers let out at 3:30, but she did not leave until 4.

The basketball team took Patrick under their wings; they taught him everything they knew – not only about basketball, but girls, also.

In the beginning, Patrick was fascinated and impressed. But, as he saw his friends victimized by schemes and plots, he devised a shell that nobody would ever penetrate.

Mary had to admit this was a welcomed change in her sister. Always concerned, yet cautious, the eldest sibling smiled.

"Oh, come on, Cissy, you're acting like a teeny-bopper. Calm down; now start from the beginning, slowly."

Catching her breath, "I need y'alls help; I'm working in Mr. Donovan's campaign and was made chairperson of the Fund-Raising Committee."

Before she could finish her request, Vance and Corneilius knew what was next.

Surprisingly, Mary was the first to speak.

"Cissy, you know the schedule around here; right now, everybody needs rest. You and your promises! I, certainly, hope you haven't written a check that someone else is suppose to cash."

Though spoken lovingly, the words were firmly stated.

"Mary, I wouldn't dare!"

"Then, how can we help you?"

"Honestly, so suspicious! But, I do wish everybody would accompany me to meet Mr. Donovan. Who knows? It could be that you'll volunteer, too. So, can I depend on it? Imagine the publicity that would be involved, from which all could benefit!"

Vance emerged, "I'm with you, Cis; I'm not doing much, these days, beyond practice.''

Running over to deliver a hug and a kiss, Cissy acknowledged appreciation. Even if nobody else would, Van, by himself, could have the same effect on Patrick's campaign.

Before now, Cissy had shown no particular interest in her family's talent. In keeping with social amenities, she said and did enough to prevent being, obviously, unenthusiastic.

Cissy Coan loved her family, but she had encountered such turmoil that the lady was about to label herself a life-time loser. And, if you don't like yourself, it's impossible to like anyone else. Everything she touched "turned from sugar to shit," as she put it.

In high school, Cissy was popular, but not as much as Catherine January. Christine was the quieter of the three. In fact, Catherine and Cissy lost their virginity the same night, at "The Path."

In those days, Cissy didn't believe in "beating around the bush." That night, she left off proper clothing. Though she had yet to complete the act, Cissy was very familiar with petting. (The drive-in was always a good place for getting started).

Her companion kept her intimately involved most of the night. Growing weary, all Cissy could concentrate on was whispers coming from the front. Catherine sobbed as her lover triumphed.

Soon, Cissy returned her attention to her partner; he was doing something strange – fireworks went off!

After meeting Cissy's politician, Mary decided to become better acquainted with the man, as well as the situation.

The night Patrick Donovan declared his platform, publicly, the entire Brown family was present. So were Marvin, Amanda, Lisa and Barney.

"…and so, ladies and gentlemen, if I had to choose just one main concern of mine – as a Christian, a person, a man, a Negro and politician, I say there must be 'Unity in the Black Community'."

The crowd cheered and yelled "victory" for the young politician for several minutes.

Patrick continued, "And, when I'm elected…."

The crowd interrupted with cheers, again.

"I shall do all that's within my jurisdiction to make this goal attainable. I want to repeat what I said – this GOAL attainable. The main difference between a goal and a dream is that one is thought about; the other is sought after. Unity, in our community, will be sought after."

Again, the crowd cheered, a passer-by would think the Falcons had come through in the last minute of the fourth quarter.

"Black people have never, really, been given the true story behind so many things that have occurred in America. And, it's so important that all people know history as it, factually, happened. Otherwise, there's no relevance in teaching the subject. Let us, as leaders and teachers, remember that Christ, the <u>Master</u> teacher, taught <u>TRUTH."</u>

By this time, some of the indigent whites, from Flat Hollow (a declining community) strolled by. They could be heard mumbling accusations of Donovan either being a "Communist, or spy, or one of 'them troublemakers' from Atlanta."

The oration continued.

"The truth, my lovely constituents, <u>must always be told.</u> That is the <u>only</u> way to free minds and break the shackles of poverty and oppression."

The thundering applause could be heard for miles around. Shortly, the local sheriff began circling.

"That is the main difference between the Bible and any other book that exists – the TRUTH. One of the most distorted tales in history is that of how dear, kind-hearted Abe Lincoln freed the slaves, as brought out in various textbooks and the media. But, Lincoln's personality is not the issue. My issue, now, is what we are doing, where we're going, and how we are dealing with each other daily."

By now, deputies could be seen, posted at conspicuous spots. Some of the town's Anglo-Saxons, actually, thought Donovan was leading a conspiracy. All he was guilty of was trying to win a seat on the all-white school board.

Emphatically, Patrick proclaimed:

"Slavery was the major issue in the presidential election campaign of 1860. The Fugitive Slave Act of 1850 and John Brown's raid on the arsenal at Harper's Ferry, had divided the nation. The Southern states insisted that the federal government had no authority to interfere in their domestic institutions, by which they meant slavery. They also wanted to see slavery established in the new Western territories of the United States."

Fletcher, an accused bi-sexual, knew exactly what it would take to buy off his fat friend. Slightly nodding his head, chewing tobacco, and one hand on his sawed-off shotgun, Sheriff Beems bustled through the area.

"Abraham Lincoln was the candidate, ladies and gentlemen, of the Republican Party…He condemned the extremism of the Northern abolitionists, and he took seriously the threats of the Southern states to secede from the union. Lincoln considered slavery to be 'a moral, a social, and a political wrong, but he did not take a strong stand against it…The Civil War began on April 12, 1861, when the Confederate forces attacked Fort Sumter in Charleston Harbor."

The crowd was so attentive that they had not noticed the investigation – nobody but Fletcher and Barney.

"The fighting lasted for four years – until May, 1865. It was one of the bloodiest wars in the history of our country."

Though Donovan was a few years younger than Cissy, she found herself wishing, deeply, that she could withdraw her request to

Christine Rosser. Cissy was bursting with pride. She remembered a conversation they'd had earlier about war, (either verbal or physical) being our only effective means of communication.

"The only progress we're making, in this Intellectual Era, is in the field of computers. But, what about mankind's relationships among themselves – each other…," her friend had questioned.

On the platform, Donovan fired away.

"President Lincoln made it crystal clear that his major goal was to save his own behind, just like so many white and Black people today."

The crowd roared with laughter.

"Only concern with saving the Union – not to free the slaves,… in a letter to Horace Greely, the abolitionist, on August 22, 1862, Lincoln wrote:

'My paramount objective is to save the Union…If I could save the Union without freeing any slave, I would do it; if I could save it by freeing all the slaves, I would do it; and if I could save it by freeing some and leaving others alone, I would also do it…'

Lincoln proposed a plan to free the slaves over a period of years. The government was to pay the slave owners for their losses, and the freed Blacks were to be sent to another country, preferably one in South America.

That story, my people, is just one truth that has long since been distorted. If we expect to be effective in our world, tomorrow, we must begin, today, teaching truth. Believe it, or not, that is a responsibility. And, again, I say when I'm elected..."

The crowd exploded in cheers for several minutes.

"Don't be afraid of opposition and criticism. It was the support of the Black community that was a major factor, six weeks ago, that won the election of Lionel Wilson, the first Black mayor of Oakland."

"I will, first, serve your needs as a community of individuals; and, secondly, I shall fight for truth to be imparted to our children, our precious future. Thank you, and, please, get some refreshments and brochures..."

To say that Donovan was received with a warm applause would be the understatement of the century. This young man had been a history teacher since he graduated, with honors, from the University of Georgia, in 1970. And, he began teaching in Springfield two years prior to this election.

With the same dynamic persuasion as with Cissy, Patrick Donovan impressed Corneilius, as well. All the Browns were captivated.

As the crowd scattered and mixed, Fletcher disappeared, and so did Sheriff Beems. Barney Blue just happened to be in the wrong place at the right time.

That evening, Cissy put forth special effort to unite her family with Patrick Donovan. She succeeded, though no extra effort was needed. The group gathered in the Brown's rehearsal room for drinks and conversation. The head of household was jubilant, having previously been described as a "hard nut to crack."

"I have no love lost in <u>any</u> politician, but you sound like my kind of man. All this play-acting is outdated; that's why I'm thinking of banning my family from the Church," exclaimed the gracious host.

"I understand exactly what you are saying, Mr. Brown, and I agree, to an extent," responded the young politician.

At that point, everybody tuned in to the conversation; Vance even ceased concentrating on his chess game.

Donovan continued.

"However, Black unity got its start during slavery, in the Church. Excommunicating ourselves, physically or mentally, can only add to current confusion."

Having recently established himself as a learned, interested, and concerned person, the group listened in awesome pleasure.

"I read someplace that 'the Church is the greatest influence in a Community. Therefore, it needs your support. The Church is one of the oldest established institutions throughout the world...it makes for A better City – A better Town – A better People. The Church represents a group of people like you and me. Its mission is to build Body, Soul and Spirit. It starts with the children...'"

Lisa rose, applauding, "Hear ye, Hear ye!"

"Pardon me; I'm afraid I'm true to form – a politician at heart. I, certainly, didn't accept your invitation to lecture you..."

Corneilius interrupted, with one hand on Donovan's shoulder.

"Son, if all our visitors came to share as you are doing, this household would be much more relaxed."

The family rendered individual gestures of agreement.

"After all, Mr. Donovan, the successful man is he who is able to persuade the crowd that he has something that they want, or that they want something that he has," Mary interjected.

"First of all, my name is Pat or Patrick to each of you; anybody who speaks words of wisdom with such ease should be on a first-name basis with kings and queens."

Everybody laughed, including Russ, who is usually solemn and in deep thought. He was concerned about his friend, who drifted off into the crowd at least forty-five minutes before this group left. But, to Russell, Donovan was, somehow, different – more sincere.

"Mist-er-uh-Patrick, you are a dynamic orator; you move people. Few speakers succeed who attempt merely to make people think – they want to be made to feel. People will pay liberally to be made to feel or to laugh, while they will begrudge a sixpence for instruction or talk that will make them think," the young Stone remarked.

Smiling and nodding, vehemently, Mary expounded, "The reasons are palpable and plain; it is heart against head; soul against logic; and soul is bound to win everytime."

By this time, Van had claimed victory in chess and was anxiously awaiting an opportunity to voice his opinion of the up-and-coming school board member. Earlier, he had indicated to Cissy that he would support her interest.

"Right on, Ma, and effective speakers utilize the same tools Patrick did tonight; they play upon men's sympathies, their prejudices, their hopes, their fears, their desires, their aversions."

At that moment, a car door slammed. Tires screamed and footsteps were heard, rapidly, approaching the side entrance to the lower level. Silence fell over the congregation of jubilance. Fortunately, the younger Browns had retired for the evening. It was Corneilius who discovered the "fox in the hen house" to be Blue.

"Well, gang, it's victory at the polls in four weeks! Ladies and gentleman, the first Black man to win a seat on the Springfield Board of Education, Mr. Patrick Donovan."

"Hold on, Mr. Blue. While I appreciate the confidence you have in me, I'd like to inquire as to whether or not you are privy to a bit of information that we aren't."

"Everybody in here knows Fletcher, I'm sure. But, what you don't know is he and our fat ass sheriff are lovers! Yep, I caught them dead to right – about an hour ago."

Everybody's mouth fell open, and their eyes bulged. Their previous conversation ceased, immediately; a new revelation had swept through the room, annihilating the low of wisdom and creativity. Physical energies faded.

Though dumbfounded, Cissy managed to walk her friend to his car as they fought to converse, normally, about the scheduled meetings and speaking engagements. Thus far, neither had made any intimate overtures.

Patrick was only dependent on Cissy's energy, resources, and aggression for a "breakeven" campaign, financially.

Later that night, Lisa prodded Blue for details of the intimacies shared between Fletcher and Beems.

"But, Barney, I've heard that men satisfy each other in any number of ways – two in particular. Please, please, tell me, which were they doing?"

"If I tell you, do you promise to go to sleep – no more questions?"

"No, honestly; I promise – no more questions."

"Both."

Book VII

THE CONTROLLING DEVICE

Patrick and Cissy were in the back seat; Corneilius and Van were up front. The foursome traveled ten miles east to a youth development center where Donovan was scheduled to speak. Every six months, a different group of boys, depending on their tenure and behavior, was released to return to their families. But, before departing, the lads would undergo various phases – the last one was talking to an "outsider," who is a productive member of society, preferably a young male. This time, Donovan was chosen. He accepted, graciously; after all, this is the type of student he felt closer to in the classroom.

Patrick had grown up near West Vine, which is a village that is controlled by the housing authority. He saw, firsthand, how children are victimized, initially, by their environment, how hosts of men who had been proud, once, drift from Dr. Jekyll to Mr. Hyde in a span of fifteen minutes, whose days were dreams, and tomorrows, visions.

As soon as this foursome had been ushered through two outside iron doors that buzzed and clanged, outrageously, after entrance, a young man yelled, "Hey now, Mr. D. – like, what it is, Brother Man?"

"Hey, Buck!"
It was Simon McKnight, a former student.

As they were being led to a conference room, into which only a special key gave entrance, Donovan requested a private meeting with Buck.

"So, how long do you have in here, Buck, and what are your plans when you leave?"

"Oh, chicken feathers, Mr. D., you'a always so serious – I got three mo' monts."

A slight smile (more like a friendly acceptance overture) came over the former
Professor's face as he recalled his days in the classroom with Simon and the gang.

"You've always had a head on your shoulders, and I hate to see you throw your talent
away."

"Ah, man, this place is jive, like skools and them phony prince-puls' and teach-uhs…"

Donovan interrupted.

"I was your teacher, Buck, and we all got along real well. I tried to, also, be your friend."

"Yeah, I know; you waz purty strait'. I'm just laid back, right now; I'm gittin' my ack together. But, I ain't kissin' no butts, Mr. D."

"And well, you shouldn't, Buck. But, there are rules in every society, and, sometimes, all of us must give up our rights for another's wrongs…"

"It jest ain't right – the way thangs go down. I kud be in charge, here, and ev'rthang would run much smootha. Uthugh than so-called white skin, whut's the Ranger got I ain't?"

"Credit, prestige, respect, an education,…"

"Ok, ok, but...'
Again the young professor interrupted.

"I know what you mean, Buck. Again, you are right. But, what are you proving and where are you going, now? Right now? Three months from now, you'll have a fresh start, and I want to help you launch into orbit. Tell you what, tell me the person you idolize or admire the most."

Smiling and blushing, the youth responded, "Jest b'tween you and me, Mr. D., I shonuff would like to tumble a certain stallion I seen once. I like a woman wid brains and beauty. I kain't stan,' them prissy ackin' bitches who always husban' huntin'."

Again, Donovan squirmed a half-smile. This jewel of a fish had, narrowly, escaped several baited hooks, himself. And, most of the lines were being held by jealousy, greed, discontent, anxiety, frustration, fear, and, sometimes, hatred.

The juvenile continued.

"I wanna meet that bad Ange'la Davis, you know – the chick that stotted a prison revoke at San Quennin..."

Another adult interruption, this time with raised eyebrows and a stern jaw.

"Get your facts straight, Lil Bro. In 1970, Angela Davis became active in prison reform. She was particularly interested in Soledad State Prison in California. In August, 1970, guns allegedly bought by Miss Davis were used in an attempt to free some prisoners from Soledad who were in a courtroom. Shooting broke out, and the judge, several convicts, and Jonathan Peter Jackson, the brother of George Jackson, were killed. Miss Davis went into hiding. Several months later she was found in New York City. She was taken back to California where she was charged with murder. Even though she had not taken part in the shooting, police believed that she had helped to plan the event. She spent more than a year in jail before and during the trial. In June, 1972, she was found innocent. In the book, <u>If They Come in the Morning,</u> she wrote that she believed that she was imprisoned because of her unpopular political beliefs."

Slight embarrassed, but truly grateful, the bright-eyed youth retorted, "You ast whut you could do, Mr. D., - buy me that book. I dig the chick."

Another smirk.

It was very late when Vance stopped in front of Cissy's – where Patrick had left his car. The father and son waved goodnight as they started for home. Cissy invited Donovan in for a drink and a bit of relaxation. The invitation, at this hour, was most unusual, the acceptance even more.

In front of the fireplace, reposed on Cissy's twelve-foot sofa was a long, handsome, tired, aspiring politician. His eyes were closed as he massaged his own temples. The hostess

entered carrying two chilled glasses of Rose.

"Here you are, Patrick; I don't see how you do it day after day. You plow through every obstacle that's thrown in your path…"

Cissy seemed to have been bitten by Cupid and the Angel of Appreciation, simultaneously. Being somewhat discouraged, drained of any natural energies, Donovan wanted to praise his hostess for her timing. Everybody, no matter how strong or determined, needs encouragement, sometimes. He thought about his grandmother and how encouraging she was – her reference to the Third Chapter of Ecclesiastes, how for everything, there's a time and a season.

It had been a long time since he was able to compare a modern-day woman to his grandmother, or any other positive influence.

As Cissy showered her guest with unexpected revelations of her inner-self, she had (unknowingly) assumed a most revealing position as she found herself sitting in front of him.

On cue, without hesitation, one step led to another. As they kissed and embraced, Patrick discovered his hand moving, at will, over Cissy's body. When he touched her flesh, she started but did not waver her attention. The hostess followed suit, and in a matter of seconds, yet an eternity, they lay on the carpet.

"Who are you, Cissy Coan? I've known you for so long, yet we only met a couple of hours ago."

Cissy couldn't respond; she was much too busy. After all, what was there to say? She felt too much time had already lapsed talking and not doing. At this point, for the very first time in her life, she was in love. There was no doubt about it; she felt it.

"You are so soft – and sweet – gentle, yet ravishing and untamed – a perfect lady in public, a tiger in private. I like that – I love that. I want you – now. Right now."

Book VIII

BELIEF IS CRUCIAL

***

Cissy, the bottom line is love and respect, I'm convinced. While I'm not saying that every man is like Joe, I feel that he's one who appreciates getting what he needs. In turn he gives me what I need, usually, when I need it. That includes sex, which is unashamedly, a very definite and beautiful contribution to our closeness.

Perhaps if my parents had been with me longer, I wouldn't have possessed such a profound need for a Real – love relationship. And, having few friends here, Joe became my best friend, after a while.

No matter the reason, what Joe and I have discovered together, has worked, so far.

I have spent this entire day writing to you, Cissy. And, it has been fun. I've thought about many people and things of the past. Some were pleasant; others were sad; but, every single experience I've had has made me the woman I am, today. And, I thank God for my journey; I am one who, constantly, looks back and wonder "how I got over."

In closing, I shall relate an incident that occurred in Joe's office about a month ago, which made me remember Mary's warning: Believe none of what you hear, and half of what you see.

Joe's secretary, Ann, called me about noon to say that "Josef Rosser will be detained indefinitely..."

I was in a good mood, and I knew how my husband could get involved in his work. So, I concluded, accurately, that he had neglected to eat. I fried enough chicken (one of Joe's favorites) for Ann, as well.

I arrived at the office about seven-thirty that evening. Just as I blurt out, the phone rang. After five times, I crossed the room to put my tray down, wondering why nobody had answered. As I turned around, I found out.

Joe was holding Ann in his arms. I stood there, unable to move. Another startling awareness – she was undressed and caressing my husband.

As Joe grabbed both of her hands, she fought and insisted on having her way.

"Ann, this is ridiculous; remind me never to order any more wine for you. In the morning, you'll hate yourself from shame. You're a desirable woman, but, I'm not what you need."

"You're what I <u>want</u>, Josef; that's all that matters."

"Ann, you're beautiful – and naked – how much can a man take? But, I'm not keen on today's trends; oh, I love sex and all that. It's just that – well – to be honest, I saw you with Leon in the stockroom, and..."

She jerked away and began swearing.

"Wait, Ann, I'm no saint. My wife and I do all sorts of crazy things. Maybe that's part of it, too. I'm growing older, and God knows, my wife doesn't send me off sex-starved. So, it's several things – I don't know."

Mildly stated, Miss Ann gathered her clothing and skirted right pass me in her birthday suit – to the powder room.

I retrieved the chicken and went home. Joe didn't see me, and I haven't mentioned it, yet.

When my husband arrived home, only minutes after I hopped in bed, I played possum. After a shower, he eased into bed, trying to keep from disturbing me. I turned and placed a kiss on his cheek. Joe sighed and whispered, "Know anybody who needs a job? I had to let Ann go. But, meanwhile, come here, you devil."

Whatever you decide, Cissy, let me know. After I left State College, I decided to keep my fare home handy, at least (smile) So, if there's going to be a wedding, I'm prepared.

I'll be praying for you.

All I know is how nice it is to share real love.

Yours friend always,

Chris

Book IX

THE AWAKENING

When Heart Hears

Awake, children of the King;
Arise, and do your thing.
March to the tune of victory!
Step to the beat of memory.

For, it is in pardoning
That we are pardoned.
It is in loving
That we are loved.

Easter, an opportunity, a brand new day,
Put the Master Teacher on worldly display;
Tis Divine Purpose for each life –
No matter the mystery, not even the strife.

As tests come due, strength will live
In exposed minds, there to give
Hope for tomorrow, Truth for today,
Smiles for the future; lies fade away.

But, I am no instructor,
Nor am I a prophet of Olde;

I know nothing
Of a raging sea:
I know of nothing
But things about me.

Dispell the myths; accept your role –
No matter the distance, pursue your goal.
As we live and breathe, success is in inches,
And, so we should impart-
It is the sermon lived that reaches the heart.

Exhausted in triumph, abundance flows,
When heart inherits wisdom, each direction glows.

***

Springfield's current library was quite antiquated in structure, but its materials were up-to-date, basically, because the Stone children had been educated there. Allen provided perpetual funds and resources in his will.

The Librarian was May Belle Beems, wife of the local sheriff. May Belle had lived in a wheel-chair for the past eleven years; so, Cissy helped out four hours a day.

Rumor had it that she fell down a cliff at the edge of town, near the curve where Chris' parents were killed. Only, May Belle was not in a car when her accident occurred.

She had trailed her husband from "The Path" to this location because Fletcher's mother had telephoned an alert of certain conduct between her son and the prominent sheriff. Fletcher was only a senior in high school, and the mother intended to use that point in a much less subtle way if this rendezvous were not terminated, immediately.

Sheriff Beems and his wife argued at the edge of a cliff; May Belle lost her balance and fell. She was hospitalized for eight weeks; afterwards, her prognosis indicated confinement to a wheel chair for the rest of her life.

"I take it you were campaigning, again, last night, Ms. Coan; your eyes are sparkling and your cheeks are rosy. You must've seen that young man."

"Last night, Mrs. Beems, I discovered love, for the very first time. And you know what? I've been married two times – two times!" Cissy held up two fingers.

May Belle was drinking coffee and smiling. She had always been fond of Cissy, but, somehow the young lady seemed to be fighting an eternal war with the world. Sipping from her cup, and peeping over her glasses to see Cissy's expression, "And, I've been married twenty-five years to the same man, whom I've never loved."

The young assistant whirled around with tears accumulating in her eyes. Compassion was something new for Cissy, and she found herself sobbing.

"But, how did you do it – Stay so long with a man and not love him?"

"Eleven years ago, I had a choice."

This conversation ceased; both women were fully aware of the intensity of the situation. The telephone rang; Cissy answered.

"Good morning, Springfield Library."

Mrs. Beems resumed her morning duties, which included opening the mail. She noticed her assistant avoiding eye contact.

"That was your husband; he's bringing a detective, from out of town, to dinner."

About to walk away, Cissy could contain herself no longer. She told her trusted employer how much change had come over her since Donovan had come into her life. How she saw things differently, now.

"If you close your eyes, you can see what you want to see. But, if you want to <u>know</u> what's really there, open them."

Going over and taking Mrs. Beems' hands, she said, "If your handicap is the only thing that's keeping you tied and imprisoned, you don't have an excuse for staying there. You're so sweet, and kind, and nice; I don't want you to be unhappy."

"But, I'm not unhappy, Cissy. I've found a peaceful and comfortable way of life, which is all some people need. You know what they way about a Virgo's perfection quests."

Both women laughed, as May Belle continued.

"I believe my husband is happy, too. I don't think I ever would've found a man I could wholly love; I got tired of searching and settled for a man who was able <u>and</u> willing to give me what I said I wanted. And, he settled for someone to play the role and accept it."

After having spent years next to this strong-willed, honest and efficient woman, Cissy knew May Belle Beems was sincere. Thus, the conversation ended, today and forever.

Mrs. Beems handed her aide a letter; it was from her best friend, Christine Rosser. The envelope was so thick that Cissy decided to wait until she got home before reading it.

Book X

ON DECIDING

Not understanding why, initially, Cissy arrived at her sister's with steaks and wine; she felt happier and more peaceful than ever before.

Pleased, but inquisitive, Mary welcomed her baby sister with open arms and heart.

"What's the occasion? Do I hear wedding bells?"

"No, not yet, but I'm hopeful. However, there is a special occasion – I've found myself, Mary! I feel good on the one hand and dumb, on the other. After all these years, I've been on a mad search to find what was already inside of me."

Cissy and Mary embraced and cried, uttering confessions that were inaudible to prospective eavesdroppers. The sisters knew that each bore equal value, as well as enlightenment.

Mary listened, attentively, as Cissy related the four hours of events and conversation at the library. But, the older sibling remembered their grandmother's bottom line when deciding on a mate; so, she shared it with her sister.

"If a man respects his mother, he'll respect his wife," and "you've got to be 'evenly' yoked."

Later, Cissy was browsing through a magazine, waiting for Donovan to meet her for dinner at the Brown's.

She read, "If your time with the family is limited, concentrate on really being there when you are at home."

Thinking: Hmm, this piece of advice may come in handy, soon. Cissy continued reading.

"Tune in to your spouse and children so you can identify a genuine plea for special time with you when it occurs, and be prepared to make it happen. Let family sharing

spring from normal activities and make it a point to look at <u>and</u> listen to the people you love. Regardless of how busy you are, your family should know absolutely that for you, simply being at home and being with them is the very best part of your day."

Cissy thought: the author of this article must've been born in July, a typical Cancerian's way of thinking – mothers of the world.

Unaware that she had company, Cissy buried herself in the magazine. Suddenly, a hand squeezed her shoulder. She turned, abruptly. It was Patrick. He was about to begin caressing her, when Cissy jerked away, playfully.

"Shame on you, Mr. Donovan. Respect my sister's house."

They greeted each other with a long kiss and exchange of brief caresses.

It was time for the evening news, and the most recent visitor was anxious to hear what was going on; so, he flipped on the television.

Mary yelled from the top of the stairs.

"I'll be back in about forty-five minutes. Hope nobody's starving. The gang will be back with me; Van may call from the airport. Cis, there's wine down there but not much else. Make yourselves comfortable, and I'll see you, shortly."

There was a half bath in the area, and without warning, Cissy disappeared to perform certain ablutions in preparation for initiating a rite of celebration.

She returned and placed a filled plastic bag in her purse. Approaching Patrick from the rear, she placed her lilac scented hand over his eyes and muttered, "Guess who?"

Patrick, gently, led his mate to join him on the rattan love seat. Cissy eyed a divan over in the west corner, near a window that lent visibility to outside activities.

Anticipating more privacy and safety, the young woman led Patrick to both of her discoveries. Instantly, the reason for the earlier disappearance was apparent.

Later that evening, after such a scrumptious repast, everybody gathered to discuss political tactics and maneuvers. Before following the itinerary, Corneilius asked Patrick about his stand on "Black English."

Donovan rendered an unyielding objection to the existence of any such animal, an opinion that the public had to be cajoled into believing in "Universal Education."

"When Slavery existed, keeping them ignorant was the thing; it, simply, compounded the problems," exclaimed the aspiring board member.

"We should be working toward spiral community."

"Yeah," Vance interjected. "It's sort of like when pregnant teenagers were put out of school and not allowed to return."

Mary joined in.

"Society forgets its place, sometimes. The natural stream of things is punishment enough. What goes around comes around – in its own time."

Corneilius laughed and said, "I know that's right – crying in the middle of the night, changing diapers, wailing for nothing, throwing pots over the kitchen,…"

Playfully, Mary interrupted her husband with a tap on the head.

"All right! All right! We get the point."

They all laughed and settled down to serious business.

Lisa was awakened by a phone call from Nurse Edwards at Lady Immaculate.

"Your father is fading fast; if you wish to see him alive, again, I suggest you come right away."

Regardless of the hour, Mary had requested Lisa to inform her, immediately, of any change in her father's condition. After waking her household, Lisa did just that.

At four in the morning, three cars, filled to capacity, paraded down Highway 19, from Springfield to Lady Immaculate.

It had been almost a year since Mary had seen Allen K. Stone. So, when she saw him lying there, eyes closed, tubes running to every possible orifice, this skeleton of a man expelled all familiarity. She, almost, recoiled. However, maintaining as best she could, Mary held one of his bony hands as Lisa, gently, stroked the other.

Russell sat by his head, Blue at his feet; Corneilius, Van, and others stood around the wall. Marvin and Amanda were on either side, close to Mary and Lisa, respectively.

Stone made several attempts to talk, but the Angel of Death was persistent, at this hour. No suffering, no resisting, this giant, of his day, slipped into eternal rest.

Nurse Edwards had spent more time with Allen, alone, than any other of the hospital staff. Though known for her strict discipline, Marlene was dedicated to her work.

Recognizing this woman's inner feelings, Allen K. Stone confided in Marlene Edwards, requesting that she share the same with Lisa and Russ. On several sheets of dictation, he even managed to scribble his signature.

Two days after the funeral, Amanda joined Lisa on the patio.

"Honey, this may be a bad time, but Marvin wanted me to let you know we're moving, next week-end."

Having completely forgotten their plans and Barney's moving arrangements, Lisa sat up.

"Oh, Amanda, forgive me; I've been so into myself that I've neglected you."

Brushing her cheeks, Amanda assured her play – daughter.

"There comes a time in all our lives, no matter how unselfish we may be, that day of reckoning. You haven't neglected me, Angel. In fact, I wanted to postpone our moving date, but, Marvin's brother will be visiting, and we can use his help."

Lisa assured her faithful companion that everything would work out fine.

Before Stone's death, Russ had been, habitually, consorting with the mayor's daughter, Elizabeth. When he and Blue spoke of the union, it was like a business venture. According to last evening's discussion, she anticipated the mood of the two partners.

Realistically aware, Lisa knew she must act fast on her previous resolution. Remaining grief stricken and empty, the young woman accompanied Amanda to their game room, where Marvin, Barney, and Russ were bowling. Lisa asked Barney for a private meeting.

"You guys think you're smart, but by the same token, I ain't so dumb."

"Hold on, Li, what's your wild assumption this time?"

Discussing Russell and Elizabeth's relationship, the couple discovered that they had begun to stroll through the flower garden. In minutes, Barney and Lisa had reached a secluded area.

"Barn, how do you feel about me?"

"What kinda question is that, Lisa Stone? You know I love you."

"Love me? Love me, how?"

"How many ways can you love?"

Meanwhile, they were seated in an old picnic spot, and a few traces of inhabitance remained. Lisa was sitting on a weather-beaten table; Barney stood at her side, playing with fringes on the umbrella.

"Many ways, a trillion ways. I've loved you in several of them since our meeting. And, I love you in one of them, now."

Both young people avoided eye contact. As worldly as Barney was, he found himself feeling uncomfortable. Since his arrival in Springfield, he had been involved in several affairs (Constance Stone was his first), but all were void of feeling. Speechless, Barney wondered if he should kiss her, or …

Lisa had always been magnetic, yet shy, with the young men in and around this expanding town. Somehow, none were quite her type. Her need for companionship was great, but most of her male acquaintances bore her silly – all except, Barney Blue.

Dusk approached, and Lisa knew they would be missed and sought, soon. But, before they rejoined the family, the young woman wanted to know once and for all…

"Barney, hold me; kiss me –touch me."

Without hesitation, Barney complied. So many thoughts crossed his mind that he was perplexed as to which took priority. He thought, finally: What the hell, talk is cheap anyhow.

Barney found himself possessing her in a state of oblivion. Chills shook his body in an unbelievable fashion.

As he was straightening his attire, Lisa whispered, "Don't you want me, again?"

Both lost count of their encounters, but each was relieved and ecstatic that a meeting of the minds came forth, simultaneously.

Embraced and propped against a tree, Lisa asked, "So, when's the wedding, Superman?"

Barney smiled, lowered his face and held his love closely.

"Typical female."

When Mary told Cissy about the double weeding: Russ and Elizabeth – Barney and Lisa, she took a seat and felt breathlessly shocked.

Book XI

DUE CROSS AND CROWN

Recuperating from what she'd heard earlier, Cissy shared the news with Patrick when he picked her up from Mary's. The family trailed in the van. The Brown Clan was scheduled for a tour, which included Jamaica; they were leaving from Donovan's headquarters for the airport at eleven.

"Do you think you'll ever remarry, Cissy," querried Patrick, as they rode along, listening to the radio.

"Sure, if the right man comes along."

"And, how will you know?"

"As my sister said years ago, I'll know."

Cissy smiled and leaned her head back on the headrest. She began to hum with Aretha Franklin, one of her favorite female vocalists. Though blessed with a lovely singing voice, Cissy Coan never pursued a career in music.

After Patrick and Cissy arrived at her place, the board-member hopeful reached over the seat for a bottle of champagne.

"The way I see it, this is the last night we'll have alone, before election night. I brought this special bottle to toast victory at the polls, and –our engagement."

Fighting to catch her breath, Cissy assisted her finance in placing her ring. Uncontrollable tears stained her cheeks as she thought: Cissy Donovan.

She found herself so overwhelmed that Patrick had to spend the night to keep her calm enough to sleep.

Next morning, the radiant couple set the date for the day after election returns. Victorious or not, Patrick needed rest; he figured a honeymoon would keep him confined.

They agreed to work in blood tests the next day, while following their schedules. Since neither wanted an elaborate wedding, Cissy's plans were minimal.

When she arrived at the library, May Belle Beems didn't ask any questions. She didn't need to.

Sensing the young woman's excitement, "Cissy, please, for your sake and mine, take the rest of the morning off. Go get your blood test, or pick out your dress; do something – just get out of here."

Stopping to give the woman a hug, the young assistant sped from the library to her blood test. As she waited, Cissy rambled though her purse for a match.

"Oh my God – Chris' letter!"

After the first paragraph, "Ms. Cissy Coan? Follow me, please."

Book XII

SEASON FOR THE BUTTERFLY

Vance was backstage fidgeting with a shoelace. It was their last night in Jamaica. Afterwards, the group was scheduled to start their one-nighters- the Big Apple, then on to sunny California. After St. Louis, it was Atlanta. And, the following twenty-four hours led into Election Day in Springfield.

"I sneaked back here, Van, because I had to see you; I've been in the audience every night. Are you remarried, yet?"

Vance jerked his head up so hard that he almost threw himself on the floor. Impossible! It was Maria.

Approaching her with wide open arms, the young Brown stammered.

"Th-th-this time, I don't dare hope, but you look the same. How have you been? How many children do you have?"

Returning his hug, Maria responded.

"No fair, you don't answer a question with a question."

"No, my lovely, I'm not remarried."

Leading his visitor to a couch, "Now, answer my question."

They sat down, holding hands.

"None – and, no husband, either."

"Five minutes to show time!"

As the ballroom filled with well-wishers, campaign workers, family, constituents and party-goers, Cissy, Lisa, Elizabeth and Mary placed hors d' oeuvres. Russ and Barney stocked the bar. Marvin tested the microphones and speakers for late dancing, while his brother set up screens for easy viewing of returns.

Patrick had not arrived; he and Fletcher were down at City Hall. Fletcher had been one of Patrick's poll watchers.

The Brown Clan, as well as Corneilius, was home, sleeping. They were to perform for Donovan, and their recent extensive tour had prevented early arrival.

In one of the town's three taxi-cabs was an unexpected well-rested guest, pioneering to the motel to join her new mother-in-law, Van's new bride, Maria Brown.

As the noise and excitement began to diminish, Cissy stole away to a private corner to read, finally, the letter from Christine.

Just as she completed the last line, Patrick appeared. They greeted each other with a long and arousing kiss. Cissy felt the paper fall from her hand. She thought: I know, Chris, I know.

As the gang gathered to watch the returns, Patrick, in his anticipation, toyed with Cissy's engagement ring.

The soon-to-be Cissy Donovan smiled: Oh God, Chris, how I know! I know that this is my season.

THE EPILOGUE

"Tis truly wonderful to fear not, to sleep each night and dream not, to love someone and doubt not."

About the Author

Dr. Pat Dugas is a retired high school English teacher, who enjoyed 33 years in the classroom, helping to shape and mold young minds to be productive citizens. She was born to the proud parents of Deacon Julius and Mother Ella M. Brown, who met and married at Greater Mount Calvary Baptist Church, Atlanta, Georgia, under the pastorate of the late Dr. B. J. Johnson, Sr. Dr. Dugas graduated from Fort Valley State University and Life Christian University/ Living Water Bible Seminary. Currently, she serves as an Associate Minister at Beulah Missionary Baptist Church, under the tutelage of Rev. Jerry D. Black, Decatur, Georgia.